Moose, the Old Shop and Jericho

By Paul Curtis

Published by Brindledog Books

To Frances

Love from

Paul

X

Moose, the Old Shop and Jericho

Published by Brindledog Books
13 Adelaide Court
30 Copers Cope Road
Beckenham
BR3 1TT
paulcurtis973@btinternet.com

© 2008 Paul Curtis

First published 2008

Cover: Original graphic: Paul Curtis. Design: Will Bruce.

Printed and bound in Great Britain by:
TJ International Ltd
Padstow
Cornwall

ISBN: 978-0-9561260-0-9

Acknowledgements

This book has taken a lot longer to write than I ever could have imagined and along the way I have had a lot of help, some direct, some indirect. Now, at last, I can say thank you.

Issek Barr, Mira Curtis-Barr, Sygall Barr

Peter and Frances Curtis
Abigail and Adrian Pennial
James and Aimi Curtis
Emily Curtis
Valerie Baker
Maureen Thurston
Mark Butterfield and Charlotte and Jack
Paul and Charlotte
Anne Orange
Anne and Katy
Anne Curtis
Gordon McClean
Debbie Warren
Sheila and Doug Warren
The Dewar Clan
Maurice Linke
Susan Ellis
La-Donna Preston and Maureen Springbett
And finally, thanks to Gerry Duggin for bullying me (oh, and editing the book)

For Lyn

Moose, The Old Shop and Jericho

CHAPTER 1

He was lying in the gutter amongst a pile of black rubbish bags. It was dark, and an icy wind raked rain across the empty city street. Some way distant but coming towards him were a gang of bin-men. Hooded and faceless they marched to the steady rhythm of their swishing brooms and the shrill scrape of their shovels. Helpless he watched as step by step they advanced. Frozen with fear, he knew they were coming to get him.

Jerry woke up. His eyes snapped open and for the first few blissful moments of consciousness he felt nothing other than relief that, once again, it had only been a dream. Then, without warning, a hammer inside his head swung against his temple, rattling his eyes and forcing from him an involuntary howl of pain. He clamped his eyes shut and pressed the heels of his small paws into his forehead.

When the pain had settled down, at least to a degree that didn't make him want to saw his own head off, he opened his eyes again. Cautiously he slid his eyeballs left and right and surveyed his surroundings. He was lying behind the counter of old shop amongst a debris of empty beer cans, crisp packets and take-away food containers. A dim memory of lots of beer and chicken curry drifted into his muddled brain.

He was confused. He knew he shouldn't be where he was and he knew he needed to sort this out, but thinking made his head hurt, so he just lay still while the hammer in his head continued trying to knock a hole in his skull.

CHAPTER 2

The Watson family, Mr and Mrs Watson and their two children Thomas and Hannah, came to a halt outside the old shop.

"We passed this place ten minutes ago, George," said Mrs Watson. "We're going round in circles."

It had been George Watson's suggestion that they take a shortcut after leaving the underground station and he was fairly sure his wife was right in saying that they were lost. However he had no intention of admitting it.

"We may have passed a similar shop but we haven't passed this one," he said. He stood on the street corner looking left and right, trying to give the impression that he was a man who had everything under control.

Mrs Watson looked at the shop's shabby doorway and grimy windows. "George I hardly think that there are two shops like this one."

George Watson gave the shop a cursory glance and noted that it was indeed the shop that they had passed earlier. It also crossed his mind that located as it was in a most fashionable part of North London the shop had considerable investment potential. Business was never far from George's mind. "Now I think we need to turn to the right here," he said.

"George," said Mrs Watson trying to keep calm, "we have been wandering around for nearly twenty minutes." She looked at her watch. "The Antique Fair will open in ten minutes and if we carry on like this we'll be lucky to get there before it closes. Can't we just find our way back to the High Street and start again?"

Mr Watson ignored her and continued surveying the streets. He was hoping someone might come along who could tell him where they were but, not surprisingly, at ten to nine on a chilly Saturday morning, the street was deserted.

"Oh for goodness sake George, just admit that you're lost," said Mrs Watson. "Then perhaps we can get out of here and get a cup of coffee."

"I am not lost," said Mr Watson crossly, "I'm simply getting my bearings. Or at least I'm trying to in between listening to you nagging me which, I might add, is pretty rich considering it was you who insisted on coming on the underground instead of in the car."

"But George we both agreed that it would be pointless bringing the car. It's two weeks before Christmas. You know what the traffic will be like and you know how cross you get in traffic jams. Surely we should turn left, we turned right when we passed this shop before."

Mr Watson heaved a deep impatient sigh. "We couldn't have turned here before Angela, because we haven't been here before, this is a totally different street and that is a totally different shop. Now if you would just keep quiet I might be able to think."

Thomas and Hannah knew from experience exactly where this kind of situation could lead. Their father might at any moment lose his temper, the result of which would be them going home to suffer a weekend of icy silence.

Thomas moved away from the group and took up a position by a lamp post some yards away. Hannah moved to follow him but the hostile glance he shot in her direction, before turning his back and conspicuously studying his iPod, made it clear that she should stay away.

At fourteen Thomas's life was a permanent sulk. He hadn't wanted to come on this outing in the first place and couldn't actually think of anything less cool than trailing around an antique fair with his parents, except perhaps

4

having his nine-year-old sister tagging along with him.

Hannah backed away. Feeling slightly awkward she started to pace around aimlessly. A few yards away her parents were now conducting an ill-tempered conversation. Her father, as usual, was getting   angrier and louder. Hannah wandered towards the old shop and stared listlessly into the dim, dirty window scanning it for something of interest. There was nothing.

The drab walls were covered with faded crepe paper and against the back wall lurched some rickety shelving, along which were scattered a few dusty cardboard boxes and old display cards. Hannah stepped back and looked up at the faded sign. The lettering, barely legible against the ancient peeling paintwork, read "The Toy Shop". Surprised, Hannah looked back into the grubby window. Well there were certainly no toys here now. In the doorway she noticed there were two bundles of newspapers bound up with blue tape. Hannah guessed the shop was actually a newsagent, although she could easily have believed that the place had been shut down and deserted for a hundred years.

With nothing else to do, and because she was desperate to keep her mind away from what was going on with her parents, Hannah started counting the dead flies that littered the floor of the shop window. She counted slowly and played a game she often played – pretending she had a friend with her, her best friend, with whom she shared all her secrets. In the background her father's voice was becoming more heated. Hannah tried not to listen and whispered to herself, "if I can count a hundred flies, I'll get a real best friend."

Still sprawled behind the counter, all Jerry wanted to do was to go back to sleep; that one place where his hangover didn't exist. But that was proving to be impossible. Much to his irritation some people had decided that right outside the shop was a good place to have an argument.

"Gits," he muttered to himself.

Groaning, he eased himself into an uncomfortable slouch and immediately wished he'd stayed lying down, Every bit of him hurt horribly. He felt sick too, a feeling not helped by the overpowering smell of the remains of last night's chicken curry. Cold and congealed it lay in a tin foil tray beside him. He pushed it away in disgust.

His cotton wool dry mouth craved moisture so he picked up one of the various lager cans scattered around him, jiggled it, and was mildly pleased to find that it was maybe a quarter full.

Jerry drank the lukewarm contents down in one go and, feeling about one percent better, started poking around in an ashtray. He lit the largest cigarette butt he could find. This made him cough noisily and caused the thump rate of the hammer in his head to go up a couple of gears. He stubbed out the cigarette and letting out a deep agonised sigh flopped backwards spread-eagled on the floor like a beached starfish. Gazing at the ceiling through gritty burning eyes Jerry promised himself two things: one he would never drink or smoke again (he'd made that promise to himself many times before and never kept it), and two, if he ever got the chance he would hit whoever it was outside on the pavement making such racket over the head with a house brick.

He closed his eyes, took three or four deep breaths and tried to create a calm space. But then came the sound of a slamming door from the flat above the shop followed by heavy, plodding footsteps on uncarpeted stairs. Jerry's eyes popped open. He looked at the wall clock which to his horror showed the time to be nearly nine-o-clock, and that

6

meant that the old man must be on his way down to open up the shop. A wave of panic engulfed him.

Disregarding the thumping in his head and his churning stomach, Jerry scrambled unsteadily to his feet. He immediately felt dizzy and fell forward surfing a slick of curry sauce across the floor. Unleashing a volley of foul language, he picked himself up and staggered towards the raised doorway that led to his hideaway in the shop window. Panting heavily, he paused for a while before attempting the awkward climb through the small door. Luckily the old man's journey down the stairs was always a slow process, so Jerry had a precious couple of moments to get his breath back. He waited until he heard the key turning in the shop door and then, after a brief but violent struggle, managed to haul himself up into the window. With his eyes screwed shut as pain seared through his head, he lay slumped in the back of the window.

After a few seconds his heart rate settled down and he opened his eyes. The harsh daylight was painful to look at and he blinked a few times trying to focus. Then the hazy features of a small girl staring at him from the other side of the glass swam into view. He wanted to cry. After nearly killing himself to avoid being seen by Old Jones, here he was being gawped at by an awful child. And there were others with her too; luckily though they were all facing the other way.

In the shop Jerry could hear the old man shuffling around puffing and mumbling grumpily. Despairingly he gave the situation a moment's thought and then did the only thing he could – hauled himself wearily to his feet and tottered unsteadily to his hideaway. Hannah waved at him excitedly. Jerry stuck his tongue out.

7

CHAPTER 3

"Good heavens what's all the excitement about?" Hannah's father said, "and what is it I'm supposed to be looking at?" George was standing alongside his daughter peering into what appeared to him to be an empty shop window.

"In there," said Hannah, pointing at where she had seen the bear disappear. "He's hiding in there." She was almost too excited to speak.

Bewildered, Hannah's father looked down at her. "Who's hiding?"

"The bear, a teddy bear but he isn't a toy, he's alive." She pressed her face closer to the glass and squinted into the darkness. "He went into that corner and stuck his tongue out at me."

Mr Watson turned to his wife who had now joined them. She shrugged and shook her head.

"What teddy bear?" said George.

Hannah turned towards her parents. "You and Mummy were arguing so I was counting the dead flies. Well, then something got in the window through that little door and it was a funny looking teddy bear with a little suit on." As she spoke Hannah began to feel uneasy. Her parents, she noticed, were both looking at her with identical stony expressions. Thomas was standing behind them smirking. Pluckily she pressed on. "Then he went into that corner, behind those cardboard things. That's when he stuck his tongue out, so I called you to have a look."

Hannah felt breathless from the effort to subdue the embarrassment that was starting to settle on her. For a while neither of her parents said anything; they simply stared at her and exchanged worried glances, which only added to

Hannah's discomfort. They obviously didn't believe her. But then of course why should they? She was now horribly aware that in the absence of any evidence to support her story she simply sounded ridiculous.

It was Hannah's father who broke the silence. Massaging his eyes with his thumb and forefinger, he turned to Mrs Watson. "What the bloody hell is she talking about?"

"I did see it daddy, honestly I did," Hannah said earnestly. "The teddy bear was lying in the window. Then he got up and walked over to that corner. He really did."

"Oh for God's sake Hannah, shut up," said her father.

Her mother cut in quickly, "it's because we were arguing George. You know how she hates it."

"We weren't arguing Angela, we were simply having a discussion," he replied, "and okay, I can understand that sometimes that upsets her, but it isn't any excuse for making up stupid stories."

"But I wasn't making it up, I saw it," insisted Hannah. "Let's go in the shop and ask."

Her father laughed out loud. "Are you serious? Are you really serious? What do you want me to say? Excuse me have you got any teddy bears here? Oh, and by the way I was really looking for one that walks around and sticks its tongue out. I don't think so."

Hannah shrank away from her father's sarcasm, "Well I'll ask, honestly, I don't mind."

"I'm sure you don't," said Mr Watson, "but I certainly do." He leant towards her with his face very close to hers, "and I don't want to hear another word of this nonsense. Do you understand?"

Hannah nodded.

"That's enough George, you've made your point," said Mrs Watson, stepping between them and moving Hannah away. "I think the best thing we can do if we ever want to get to this Antiques Fair, is to forget all this and see if we can find our way back to the High Street and start again. Or maybe you'd rather spend the rest of the morning standing here?"

For a few anxious moments the family watched and waited as Mr Watson paced around. He seemed to be about to explode. Hannah was afraid that he might decide that they go home and that the day would be spoiled and it would be all her fault. Eventually though, and much to her relief, he muttered a grudging: "Okay", but then turned to Hannah, "you'd better be on your best behaviour young lady or else you'll be in big trouble. Do you understand?"

Sheer frustration prompted Hannah to consider one last try but she knew she was on dangerous ground and after the shortest of pauses simply whispered, "Yes daddy."

Thomas, who was now lounging by the shop window, caught Hannah's eye and made a face. Embarrassed and feeling stupid, Hannah felt her cheeks start to burn.

"Come on darling," said Mrs Watson extending her gloved hand, "lets get off this draughty corner and see if we can actually enjoy ourselves."

With no other option left, Hannah took her mother's hand and the family moved away from the old shop and headed off in, what Mrs Watson was pretty sure, was the direction of the High Street. Hannah though had seen something fantastic, something impossible to walk away from. She had seen it. No matter what her father said she knew what she had seen. She had to come back here. She had to prove to everyone that she hadn't been making it all up. She had to prove it to herself. Desperately Hannah looked back over her shoulder just as the shop door opened and a white-haired old man dragged in the bundles of newspapers from the shop doorway.

In the window, peeping from his hidden corner, Jerry watched anxiously as the family disappeared from view. When at last they had gone he heaved a sigh of relief and snuggling into the bundle of rags that was his bed he settled down to sleep.

CHAPTER 4

Having successfully found their way out of the maze of side streets and back to the High Street, the Watson family were at last approaching the Town Hall where the Antiques Fair was being held. They were discussing Hannah.

"She does it to get attention George. Dr. Kingston said it's quite common for the youngest child to feel isolated."

"But that was a year ago Angela. She's supposed to be getting better, not worse. You heard her, it was almost as if she actually believed what she was saying."

"She has a vivid imagination". Mr Watson pondered this and then said gloomily: "You know I often wonder at what point these doctors actually say 'we thought for a while she had a vivid imagination, but actually she's a total basket case.'"

"George! It's your daughter you're talking about". "I know," he said bitterly. "Nine years old and she talks about live teddy bears prancing around in shop windows and expects us to believe her. It hardly bears thinking about." Thomas who had gleefully listened to all this as he walked alongside his sister slyly nudged Hannah. She glanced up at him. He tapped the side of his head, poked his tongue out and rolled his eyes.

"Ten past nine," Mr Watson moaned as he made his way up the Town Hall steps, "we needed to be here half an hour ago. The dealers will have had all the best stuff by now." Mrs Watson shook her head in despair and with Thomas and Hannah alongside her, followed her husband up the steps.

Much to Hannah's surprise, especially as the day had started so badly, the morning spent at the Antiques Fair turned out to be, if not exactly great fun, then at least pleasant. Thomas, always a source of annoyance, had gone off to the High Street by himself to do some shopping and when her mother decided to visit an exhibition of paintings on one of the upper floors, Hannah was left strolling around the various stalls with her father. She had stayed with him as a matter of policy; he was still quite grumpy and this was a good opportunity to get into his good books. Of course the incident at the old shop was never far from her mind but she didn't dare mention it.

As the family made their way down the busy High Street back to the station Hannah listened as her father chatted to her about the skills required to spot bargains and how to get the best deals when haggling with stall-holders. He was unusually talkative and Hannah listened attentively.

"It all boils down to psychology Hannah," he said. "Knowing how the other person is thinking. Now with that woman, all it took was a little bit of friendly chat and that was it. If I'd pushed her harder she might even have dropped her price a bit more." The woman he was referring to was a stallholder from whom he had bought two brooches. And this, Hannah suspected, was the main reason for her father's good humour. He had inspected the two brooches very carefully and spent fifteen minutes convincing the woman that he was doing her a huge favour offering her a fraction of the price that she was asking for them. Eventually she had given in.

"Are those brooches really valuable then daddy?" said Hannah.

Mr Watson grinned smugly. "Well, let's just say that they're worth a lot more than I paid for them."

Hannah thought about this for a while and then, very hesitantly, as she didn't want to upset her father, said, "but if you know they're valuable isn't that a bit like cheating?"

He laughed. "Of course it's not cheating. It's business. It's not my fault if the silly woman didn't know what they were worth and after all business is business."

"But I thought collecting antiques was just your hobby," said Hannah.

"Well yes it is, in a way," said Mr Watson. "But I still approach it in a business like manner. I apply the same principles to collecting antiques as I do to my property business – buy cheap and sell dear. That, after all, is what business is all about." He took a two-pound coin out of his pocket and held it up to Hannah. "There are two ways of looking at money," he said, "as something to spend or something to invest." He pressed the coin into Hannah's hand.

As they neared the station, the pavement narrowed and became more congested. Fearing they might become separated Mr Watson stopped to allow his wife and Thomas, who were some-way behind, to catch up with them. He peered over the heads of the crowds and saw that they were some thirty yards back looking in a shop window. He stood and waited, humming gently under his breath.

Glad of the break, Hannah let her mind wander, yet again, back to what had happened at the old shop.

She had no doubt about what she had seen, though having had time to think about it she knew that it would be pointless even considering mentioning it to her parents again. But she also knew that she couldn't possibly ignore a matter as momentous as this. While trailing around the Antique Market with her father and waiting patiently while he stopped from time to time to inspect a piece that he thought might interest him, Hannah had managed to distil her jumbled thoughts to the following: If the bear was in the window of a shop then presumably it must be for sale.

And, if that was indeed the case, there should be no reason why she, Hannah, should not buy it. Having got this much clear in her head she felt free to address the only problems that now presented themselves: namely, how and when would she be able to do this. She thought about the situation as she stood alongside her father and became miserably aware that to these problems, there seemed to be no answer.

Mr Watson was also preoccupied, not though with the same things as Hannah. He was looking forward to getting home and consulting a few of his reference books to confirm the value of the two brooches. He felt the faint thrill of excitement he always felt when he pulled off a good deal and it was because his mind was on this that he didn't notice the Big Issue vendor until he was standing directly in front of him holding out a magazine.

"Big Issue sir?" Startled, Mr Watson blinked up at a huge dread-locked man who was smiling down at him.

"Best read on the market sir, news, views and information."

George Watson hated with a vengeance all street-vendors, but he especially hated Big Issue sellers whom he described as licensed muggers. Normally he kept an eye out for just such people and took evasive action. Now though he was trapped. The man smiled down at Hannah. "Good morning young lady," he said cheerfully and kept the magazine held out invitingly. Hannah smiled shyly up at him.

Mr Watson was wondering what to do. He didn't want to buy a magazine. That would have gone totally against his principle that to give money to layabouts and scroungers was simply to encourage them. However, in this situation with the man right in front of him and with Hannah clearly expecting him to buy one, George Watson was in a very difficult position. The Big Issue vendor continued beaming his big smile while George suffered an agony of indecision.

Rescue came in the form of his wife and Thomas whom Mr Watson caught sight of milling past amongst the crowd heading towards the station. Seizing his opportunity he grabbed Hannah by the wrist and muttered, "Sorry I'm in rather a hurry." He brushed past the Big Issue vendor and whisked Hannah off towards the station where he caught up with his wife and Thomas just as they were entering the ticket hall.

His mood now soured, and he immediately started moaning about the crowds and the queues to use the ticket machines. The family ignored him. They had all heard similar tirades many times before.

Standing patiently in the queue, Hannah kept looking back to where the Big Issue seller was working. She caught regular glimpses of him through the shifting banks of people. She liked it that he never stopped smiling, but also noticed that not many people were buying his magazines and couldn't help feeling sorry for him. As she watched she half listened as her father droned on about how awful everything was. And then, quite suddenly, Hannah did something that she instantly knew she would regret. She wriggled her hand free from her father's and darted back through the crowd. From her pocket she fished out the two-pound coin her father had given her earlier and handed it to the dreadlocked vendor. Grinning broadly he gave her a magazine. "Thank you very much sweetheart," he said, and bowed graciously, waving as she disappeared back into the station.

"I despair of her sometimes," said Mr Watson.

The family were on the tube going home. Mrs Watson, doing her best to ignore her husband, sat flicking through a glossy magazine. Don't make a fuss now George," she said quietly without looking up, "we can talk about it when we get home."

Aware that his wife didn't want to discuss the matter but feeling that he couldn't let it rest, he lapsed into one of his more irritating habits of muttering to no one in particular in the hope that sooner or later someone would pick up the conversation.

"Good God, one can't even walk the streets of London without being accosted by beggars and criminals these days. What is the world coming to?" For a while he just sat shaking his head, making disapproving tutting sounds. When no one spoke he continued. "Bloody scroungers and wasters all of them. And I bet he signs on every week. No wonder I pay so much bloody tax." Mrs Watson kept her head resolutely in her magazine while Hannah stared fixedly at the floor. Thomas, as usual, was lost in the blaring racket of his iPod.

"Stick them all in the Army is what I say," he continued. "See how tough they are when they're face to face with a good old fashioned drill sergeant."

Mrs Watson gave in. "For crying out loud George," she said, keeping her voice as low as she could. "All he did was sell you a magazine. He didn't come at you with a knife." "He didn't sell me anything," said Mr Watson hastily, "I wouldn't waste my money. She's the one with money to burn." He jerked an accusing thumb in Hannah's direction. "I wish I had a job like his, just standing around taking money off people."

Hannah, who had been thinking about the incident at the old shop and trying not to listen to her father now felt obliged to defend the Big Issue man. "He didn't just take the money daddy, I bought a magazine off him."

Her father ignored this and, still addressing his remarks to no one in particular, continued bitterly, "A decent day's work would probably kill him."

"But it says here it's for homeless people daddy. He's probably saving up to buy a house," she said pointing to the cover of the magazine.

"The only houses he and his kind are interested in Hannah are Public Houses," retorted her father allowing himself a snort of derisory laughter at this joke.

"Okay George," said Mrs Watson wearily, "I think you've made your point, I'm sure Hannah thought she was doing the right thing."

"But that is the point," said George, seizing on what his wife had just said, "she doesn't think. She just does or says the first thing that comes into her head," and turning to Hannah said. "You do realise I suppose, that most of these people aren't really homeless at all? They just can't be bothered to get a job and make something of themselves." Hannah said nothing. "It's the easy way out. Hang around street corners and beg while mugs like me work bloody hard to subsidise them."

His voice had got noticeably louder and a few people further down the carriage started to glance furtively in his direction. Mrs Watson dug herself deeper into her magazine. There was very little she could do when her husband was in one of these moods.

Well into his stride now, Mr Watson started giving Hannah a lecture on the measures he would take (short of hanging) to deal with Big Issue sellers and the rest of Britain's 'great unwashed' as he called them. Hannah couldn't easily ignore her father but she did her best. Fixing her attention on the simple rail map above the dark windows on the opposite side of the carriage, she was pleased to see that the next stop was theirs. As he rambled on, describing a world of boot camps and community projects like rebuilding the sewage system, she concentrated hard on the map following the black line from their home station and counting the stations back to where they had just come from – five stops on a single straight line, not very far at all when shown that way. Once again Hannah thought of the bear and as her father's voice rattled on like the clacking train itself an idea fluttered into her head.

CHAPTER 5

Standing outside the tube station squinting in the wintry daylight Hannah wondered what to do next. She was disconcerted, almost to the point of panic. Compared to yesterday, when she had been here with her parents, everything now seemed horribly different and there were hardly any people about, which in itself she found a little unnerving. Worse than this though, for the first time it struck her that not only did she not know where the old shop was, she didn't even know the name of the street it was in. All she could be certain of was that it was in a side street not far from the High Street. But which side street? There were lots of them and it now occurred to her that the only reason they had been in that particular street the day before was because her father had managed to get them lost.

The idea that she could actually find her own way back to the old shop had come to Hannah as she studied the map on the train the day before. Shown as a straight line the journey had looked ridiculously simple. And so it had proved to be, taking a little over half an hour from her house to where she now stood. The worst bit had been waiting for the train at her home station. She hadn't liked being alone on the gloomy platform with its distant echoes and brooding ticking clock but, with that behind her, the journey itself had been easy. Now though she felt lost and the early optimism, along with her confidence, was rapidly drifting away.

Hannah surveyed the wide, litter-strewn roads that went off in all directions. None of them looked even faintly familiar. She looked at her watch, twenty to nine. Her parents were rarely up before ten on Sundays. If she turned back now she could be home by half past nine and no one would ever know that she had been away. The thought of being at home, snug under her duvet was hugely tempting. But when would she get another chance to buy the bear? She put her hand in her pocket and felt, yet again, her money; fifty-five pounds, every penny of the pocket money she had been saving for Christmas. It was small consolation that if she went home now she would at least still have that. Standing in the station entrance she wondered what to do.

The Big Issue vendor had arrived at his pitch early that morning and was sitting on his stack of magazines outside a small florist shop. He watched Hannah as she glanced anxiously around her. He had recognised her immediately as the little girl who had bought a magazine from him the day before and was rather surprised to see that today she appeared to be on her own. She looked lost and this worried him, but he waited for while before calling out to her. "Hey, little girl, over here." He waved beckoning her towards him. Startled, Hannah looked up. She was awfully pleased to see a friendly face but none the less hesitated for a second. She knew her parents would be furious with her for talking to a stranger. After a few moments thought though she trotted over to him reasoning that having already met him the day before, technically he wasn't a stranger. She knew her argument was flimsy, but right now she didn't care. "Well good morning young lady," the man said smiling broadly. "You're on your own today I see."

Hannah nodded shyly.

"You live near here?"

She shook her head and then said, "Not very far away, I've come to buy a teddy bear," adding quickly but unconvincingly. "My parents know."

"I'm glad to hear it," said the Big Issue vendor, eyeing her suspiciously, and then said. "Where are you buying your teddy bear from, the market?"

"No," said Hannah, "from an old shop," and then, slightly embarrassed, she added, "but I don't know where it is."

The big man laughed. "You seem to have a problem." He held out a giant hand and said. "My name is Moses."

Hannah shook it and feeling a lot happier she grinned and said, "I'm Hannah."

"Okay Hannah," said Moses in a very business like voice. "I guess we'll have to see what we can do to sort things out. Do you have an address for this shop?"

"No, but I know it's on a corner and it's very old, and it says it's a toy shop, but it's not. It sells newspapers and an old man works there."

Moses was a stranger to the area; in fact his very first day selling the Big Issue had been the day before. The disjointed scraps of information that Hannah was coming up with meant very little to him and it soon became clear that he wasn't going to be much help to her. Moses also worried that Hannah was alone. Contrary to what Hannah had told him, it was pretty obvious to him that her parents didn't know where she was and because of this he didn't like the idea of letting her wander off by herself. Moses was beginning to wonder what he should do. As he pondered this dilemma, a young woman carrying a large shoulder bag came along and stopped in the florist's shop doorway. She glanced briefly at both Moses and Hannah then started raking vigorously through her bag. It was the girl who worked in the shop. Moses had seen her yesterday. He had caught her eye a couple of times and smiled but she hadn't responded. She seemed to be a serious type but she was also quite pretty and having the opportunity to speak to her now didn't displease Moses at all.

"Excuse me," he said, getting up from his seat on the

magazines, "I wonder if you can help us?"

"I'll try," said the young woman, without looking up. "What's the problem?"

Moses explained the situation giving her the same sketchy and confused details that Hannah had given him. The young woman, who had not stopped looking through her bag all the time Moses had been speaking, suddenly produced a large bunch of keys and this seemed to please her. Now, for the first time, she looked up. "Okay," she said, "the shop you want is in Canal Street. It's only a couple of minutes walk from here. Just let me get this door open and I'll show you where to go."

She rattled the key fiercely in the lock, "you're the new Big Issue guy aren't you?" she said, as she wiggled the key and shoved the door with her shoulder. "Damn thing. Every morning it's the same," she said breathlessly. She wiggled the key and barged the door a couple more times but it stayed firmly shut.

"Here let me try," said Moses. He took the key from her and tried to turn it. Nothing happened. He took it out of the lock and studied it carefully. "Is this a new key?"

The woman nodded, "the old one broke."

Moses took a fat penknife out of his pocket and from an impressive array of blades and tools selected a file. Then he carefully scraped away at various parts of the key and put it back in the lock, twisted it, and the door opened.

"Well what do you know," said the woman smiling, "a genuine handyman. Well I suppose if we're going to be neighbours we'd better get to know each other. I'm Linda."

Smiling and extending his hand Moses said. "How do you do, I'm Moses and this little lady is Hannah," putting his hand on Hannah's shoulder as he spoke. "She's one of my best customers."

"Okay Hannah and Mr Moses," said Linda moving to the centre of the pavement and pointing down the High Street, "the old shop is about two or three minutes from here." She started giving Moses directions but suddenly stopped and turned to Hannah, looking at her as if some grave thought had just struck her. "Hannah, what on earth do you want to go to that old place for?"

Before Hannah could answer Moses said. "Hannah wants to buy a teddy bear."

"A teddy bear!" said Linda, "What, from there?" She laughed out loud. "But Hannah it's not really a toy shop," she said. "It's only called 'The Toy Shop' because the old guy who owns it is too lazy or crazy to give the place a lick of paint and get a new sign over the door. It was a toy shop once but that was years ago."

Moses listened to this news with mild concern. "Are you sure that you've got the right place Hannah?"

"Yes, I know it's not a real toy shop, but there was a funny looking teddy bear in the window. I saw him yesterday and he...." Hannah had been about to say he stuck his tongue out, but checked herself just in time and said. "The shop wasn't open."

Linda studied Hannah carefully. "Look Hannah the old guy who runs that place is a bit odd. Are you sure you're not mistaken?"

"Odd?" said Moses, "how odd?"

Linda looked down at Hannah then turned to Moses. "Well, for a start he hates kids."

Moses began to feel uneasy. "What do you mean, he hates kids?"

"Just that," said Linda, "he hates kids," she shrugged and then continued, "I've lived around here all my life and when I was a kid I wouldn't go near the place. Too spooky, you know dark and old. The grown ups used to go there for newspapers and my dad got his pipe tobacco from there, but even he stopped going because the old man was so rude and miserable. There are lots of stories about the old place." Then, not wishing to startle Hannah unnecessarily, she added gently. "Look, I'm sure he's quite harmless just a bit fierce, you know a bit bad tempered. But it's just so funny someone expecting to buy a teddy bear from that place." Moses thought for a while and then, turning to Hannah said. "Hannah, why don't you buy a teddy bear from the market? I'm sure you could find a really nice one there."

"Because it won't be the same," said Hannah. "The one in the old shop is a special one. I have to get it from there."

It was obvious to Moses that Hannah was quite determined to go to the shop but he was equally determined that she shouldn't go on her own. He turned to Linda and drawing her to one side said. "Look, I know I shouldn't be bothering you but I think I should go with her." He lowered his voice, "I think she's on her own and I don't feel right letting her wander around on her own."

"You don't know her?" said Linda obviously surprised.

"Not 'till yesterday. She was here with her dad. She bought a magazine from me and then she turned up at the station this morning looking lost." He shrugged. "Look I really hate to bother you but do you think you could you keep an eye on my magazines while I walk to the shop with her?"

Linda studied the big man for a moment and then looked over at Hannah. Hannah smiled.

Addressing both of them Linda said sharply. "Have you two eaten this morning?" Both Hannah and Moses shook their heads.

Linda thought for a while. "Okay we'll do it this way, I

usually have tea and toast before I start work. You guys can join me when you get back from the old shop. Moses, you bring your magazines in here and get going. But don't be long, okay?"

Moses turned to Hannah. "Is that okay with you?"

Hannah, who had already decided that she liked these people, eagerly nodded her agreement.

Moses lugged his bundle of magazines into Linda's shop and taking Hannah's hand headed off with her. She trotted happily alongside him and felt a sudden thrill of anticipation and could hardly believe that very soon, and very much against the odds, she could actually be buying the bear. But more than this she had a feeling that something big was about to happen. My goodness, she thought, what an adventure this was turning out to be.

CHAPTER 6

"Are you sure this is the shop Hannah?" They were both looking in the window. "I mean it's not that I don't believe you or anything but there doesn't seem to be anything here." Moses turned to Hannah who was scanning the window anxiously. "Maybe you made a mistake eh?"

"He's probably hiding," said Hannah absently. She had hoped the bear would be in the back of the window where she had seen him the day before but there was no sign of him.

"Hiding?" said Moses. "Yes, or fallen down behind the shelves or something, you know."

Moses didn't know, but he didn't feel like pursuing the subject. Hannah had obviously seen, or more likely, thought she had seen something in the window, and now that they were here he was quite happy to let her sort it out for herself. He felt a bit sorry that she was probably going to be disappointed but there was nothing he could do about that.

He looked down at her and with an encouraging smile, he jerked his head towards the door. "Okay, shall we go in?" Hannah suddenly felt shy. She was quite prepared to be disappointed or feel foolish but she didn't want to look foolish in front of Moses. "Moses, can I go in by myself?" He looked at her thoughtfully and almost reading her mind he nodded and said, "I'll wait here for you." Hannah took hold of the door handle and after taking a deep breath went into the shop. The doorbell gave a faint rusty ping as the door opened.

Peering into the gloom she could hardly believe that the inside of the shop was even scruffier and more run down than the outside. A single light bulb hanging from the centre of the ceiling burned dimly but its meagre glow seemed to be absorbed by the brown painted walls. The dark wooden shelves were mostly empty and the scuffed worn out floor covering was holed and cracked. It all looked incredibly old. Even the air seemed old, still and heavy with a smell of neglect. Sitting behind the counter, partially lit by a shaft of dusty daylight filtering through the back of the display window, was an old man. It was the same old man Hannah had seen the day before taking in the bundles of newspaper. He was reading. A cigarette drooped out of the side of his mouth and a plume of blue smoke snaked silently towards the ceiling. Without interest, he glanced up at her over his heavy glasses. Then, without speaking or acknowledging her in any way, carried on reading.

Hannah stood silently at the counter. After a while the old man slowly raised his head again. He looked at Hannah as if she had no business being there and, through a cloud of cigarette smoke, grunted "Yeah?" Feeling very nervous Hannah said, "Can I have the teddy bear please?" She was surprised how tiny her voice sounded. "No Telegraph," he said dismissively and settled back down to his newspaper. Already feeling that she was being a nuisance Hannah didn't like to speak again. So she waited for a while before saying, very politely, "Sorry. I meant the teddy bear, in your shop window. I'd like to buy him please."

Impatiently, the old man put his paper down and stood up. Leaning over the counter menacingly he barked. "Look I ain't in the mood to be messed about...." He was about to say more, but was suddenly seized by a violent and noisy coughing fit. Hannah watched in horror as the old man stumbled about behind the counter. His whole body was shaking and his face started to turn a deep, dangerous, red.

Terrified, Hannah pulled all her money out of her coat

pocket and threw it on the counter. "Have I got enough money?". But the old man's coughing was so loud he couldn't hear anything. Hannah half expected him to collapse at any moment. After a couple of minutes, however, the coughing slowed and eventually stopped altogether. The old man, wheezing horribly and seemingly exhausted, but with his cigarette still miraculously in place, produced a huge red and white spotted handkerchief from the pocket of his brown warehouse coat and dabbed his streaming eyes. Then he blew his nose, a process that produced an intimidating foghorn blast. After this pantomime was over, Hannah, badly shaken, asked again, "Have I got enough money?" Hurriedly she pushed the money towards the old man. Out of breath he looked down at the five and ten pound notes on the counter. His red, watery, eyes fixed on Hannah and after a moment's thought he panted, "What is it you want?"

"A teddy bear, he's in your window," said Hannah, her voice was trembling slightly, "I saw him yesterday but I think he's hidden in the corner now". Then she asked again. "Do you think I've got enough money?"

The old man's eyes flickered greedily from Hannah to the crumpled notes on the counter. He didn't have the faintest idea what Hannah was talking about and under normal circumstances he would have chased her out of the shop, but the sight of the money, which Hannah seemed quite willing to part with, made him stop and think. He eyed her suspiciously and said. "What teddy bear?"

"The one in your window, I saw him yesterday and now I want to buy him."

The old man was used to children playing him up. They usually came in gangs of three and four to buy cigarettes. He looked at Hannah and decided that she probably wasn't one of them. She was too well spoken and lacked their cocky street-wise swagger. Sensing the old mans caution, Hannah said. "He is in there, but he's behind one of those big advertising cards."

The old man feared some elaborate trick was being played on him but the money lying invitingly on the counter looked real enough. Grudgingly he decided that it was worthwhile to at least investigate.

Muttering threats about what he would do to Hannah if she were messing him about, he leaned awkwardly through the small door in the back of the window and groped around blindly for a few moments. As he struggled his face gradually took on the same dangerous hue it had earlier. Hannah watched him anxiously.

Jerry, who had been fast asleep, woke up when the dusty faded advertising cards and boxes that formed his hideaway were pushed to one side and Old Jones's disembodied arm appeared flailing around only inches from his hind paws. Jerry was just about to take evasive action when the old man's thick fingers closed firmly around his leg and he was yanked unceremoniously from the window and to his utter amazement suddenly found himself being held upside down like a prize turkey. He hung lifelessly from the old man's hand wondering what was going on.

Old Jones had had no idea that Jerry had been in the window, but neither was he surprised to find him. The truth was, that beyond the area behind the counter where he sat, the old man had very little idea of what was in the rest of the shop. His customers, such as they were these days, only ever wanted two things: cigarettes and newspapers, and these two commodities were arranged so that he could supply them without moving. He never looked in his windows and it didn't occur to him to ask

Hannah how, if the bear was hidden as she had said it was, she knew that it was there. The fact was that he was a very old man and had no curiosity about anything. And anyway, at the moment he was only interested in the money.

"Is this it?" he said as he dumped Jerry heavily on counter.

Jerry lay motionless but he eyed Hannah slyly, recognising her as the dreadful little creature that he had stuck his tongue out at the day before.

"Yes, that's him," said Hannah breathless with relief and excitement. And then again asked. "Have I got enough money?"

Old Jones picked up the notes and smoothed them out. He counted them, thoughtfully stroking his chin as if he was weighing up some vast problem. After what seemed to be an age he spoke. "Now look 'ere, he said, this 'ere is a very expensive sort of teddy bear."

Hannah's spirits sunk.

The old man continued. "Now you've just given me fifty-five pounds, right?" He held the money up for Hannah to see.

She nodded.

"Well I can't take a penny less than fifty for this bear." The old man looked at Hannah. His face was very serious.

Hannah wasn't entirely sure that, if by this, the old man meant that she could afford the bear or she couldn't, so she just nodded again.

"Right," said the old man triumphantly, "so if I give you a fiver back we're all square, right?" He slapped a five pound note on the counter with a bang that made Hannah jump and said: "Is that a deal?"

Hannah smiled and nodded eagerly while the old man slipped the fifty pounds into the same pocket he had produced the handkerchief from earlier. Now, for the first time, the old man smiled revealing a wreckage of brown teeth. "I'll find you a nice bag to put him in." Just then, the shop door pinged open and two men came in.

"'Allo Jonesy," said one of them.

The old man's smile disappeared. "Hello lads," he mumbled.

Hannah watched the two men as they strolled up to the counter. One of them looked at her, holding her gaze with pale blue staring eyes that she found a bit frightening. He was wearing a tight fitting red tee shirt and his thick hairy arms were covered in tattoos. It was very cold outside so Hannah thought he must be very tough. The other man was wearing a black leather jacket. He had a long thin pale face with dark, greasy hair that was slicked back. His eyes darted in Hannah's direction and then flicked away.

"You're a busy boy this morning Jonesy." It was the one in the red tee shirt and as he spoke he picked up the bear from the counter. "'Didn't know you were in the antiques business Jonesy." He held up the scruffy bear for his friend to see. There was a snort of sly laughter from the man in the leather jacket.

The old man also laughed, but uneasily. "Yeah, well my little friend here is a bit of a collector. She just got this valuable antique at a bargain price."

Stroking Jerry's sparse hair the man in the tee shirt turned to Hannah. He smiled at her but his scary eyes still stared. "Has he been looking after you Miss?" he said jerking his head in the old man's direction.

Hannah nodded but she needed to look away from the frightening man and turned to Jones. "Is the bear really an antique?"

"He certainly is," he said, "old as the hills that little feller is."

The man in the tee shirt handed the bear back to the old man.

"My daddy collects antiques," said Hannah.

"Does he really," said Old Jones absently. "Well he will be pleased when you take this home to him." He shuffled about behind the counter opening drawers and poking around the shelves, "I got some bags here somewhere" he puffed.

The two men were now pacing around the shop, which made Hannah feel nervous. She tried to ignore them. She hoped Moses was still outside. To cover her nervousness Hannah carried on talking. "Yes, my daddy collects jewellery and things that are really valuable, you know old things and stuff." The old man though wasn't listening. He continued bustling about behind the counter and then said, "I knew I had one somewhere." He waved a large plastic bag and was about to pick up the bear when the man in the red tee shirt stopped him.

"Jonesy," he said reprovingly, "you're not seriously going to put that valuable piece of merchandise in that scruffy old bag are you?"

Flustered the old man spluttered. "Well, yeah, I was."

The man cut him short. "What, after our young friend here has just told you all about her dad and his antiques, you're going to let her take her valuable purchase home in a plastic bag? I don't think her dad would be very impressed with that, do you?"

The man in the leather jacket suddenly appeared behind the counter and held out a key. "In the back room Jonesy there's loads of boxes out there." Old Jones hesitated for a moment before taking the key and shuffling out to the back room. "And don't touch any of the other stuff," he called after him.

With the old man out of the shop the man in the tee shirt turned to Hannah. He shook his head. "Silly old devil, he hasn't got a clue what he's doing." He tapped the side of his head with his forefinger, "I think he's losing it." He turned to his friend. "Don't you Kev. Don't you think he's losing it?"

"No doubt about it Sid," said Kev, "he's getting worse."

Sid picked up the bear from the counter and handed it to Hannah. This was the first time she had held him and was surprised and a bit disappointed that the bear felt limp and lifeless exactly like any ordinary teddy.

"I bet he didn't even give you a guarantee for this valuable item, did he?"

"No."

Sid shook his head sadly. "What do you think of that Kev? You're right you know. He is getting worse." He turned back to Hannah. "Lucky for you, me and my mate here came along or you'd have gone away with a very expensive and valuable item of merchandise and no guarantee and that would never do would it?"

"I suppose not," said Hannah.

"You suppose right," said Sid, "and I'll tell you what I'm going to do." He darted behind the counter and got a pen and notebook out of a drawer. Pushing them across the counter towards Hannah he said. "You write your name and address down here for me and I'll make sure you get a guarantee. Then if anything goes wrong you're covered like, ain't yer."

Hannah, who just wanted to get out of the shop, placed Jerry back on the counter and in her best handwriting did as Sid had asked. When she had finished she pushed the notebook back to Sid who looked at what she had written and said, "Well done sweetheart" as he tore the sheet of paper from the book and then in a low voice, as if sharing a confidence with her, "look, me and my mate we gotta go now. Best not mention this to the old man, he gets a bit upset when he forgets things, you know what I mean." He tapped his head with his forefinger again.

Hannah nodded.

Holding up the piece of paper Sid gave her a friendly wink and said "I'll get that in the post to you on Monday." As the two men left, the leather jacketed Kev called out. "Tell the old boy I'll be back for the key later." And with that they were gone.

Alone now in the shop, Hannah turned her attention to the bear. She picked him up and gave him a squeeze. He felt very ordinary. She gave him a gentle shake. The bear flopped lifelessly from side to side. She tried standing him on the counter but when she let him go he just keeled over. Hannah pulled him close and studied him carefully. He was totally lifeless. She whispered in his ear, "I'm taking you home with me. We're going to be best friends."

Even though rage and panic was flapping around inside Jerry like a room full of screaming birds he didn't move. He lay still and lifeless cradled in the little girls arms. He felt ridiculous. Frantically he went through his options and it didn't take him long to work out that, short of jumping up and running back into the widow, he didn't have any. He was trapped. The horrible reality of the situation was that he would soon be going to who-knows-where with this dreadful child and there wasn't a thing he could do about it.

The old man breezed back into the shop looking particularly pleased with himself. He was carrying a large but rather tatty looking box. He looked around, surprised that the two men had gone, and said, "They were right you know, there are loads of boxes out the back there. I think this might even be the box he's supposed to be in." He held it up for Hannah to see. She studied it carefully. The illustration on the lid showed a cute little bear dressed in a smart pale blue suit. Alongside him was the name "Jerry". He was holding a guitar. Above him, in jaunty script, was written: "The Jericho Boys, Teddy Bear Pop Group." Beneath, three other bears were illustrated. They grinned happily from the box lid, Jake, Josh and James – "Collect all four" ran the legend.

The old man shook his head. "Lord knows how long that's been out there. I really will have to have a sort out here one day." He took the bear from Hannah, stuffed him roughly in the box and secured it with a length of string.

Cramped and uncomfortable in the box Jerry wanted to scream. What was to become of him? The only life he knew was the old shop. How would he survive away from it?

CHAPTER 7

"His name is Jerry," said Hannah. She and Moses were back at Linda's shop enjoying the tea and toast she had made for them. They were studying the bear which was perched on a stool staring at them mutely.

"Do you think he's nice?" said Hannah.

There was a pause while Linda and Moses considered this question. With his scruffy, dirty clothes and ridiculous face, 'nice' was not a word that could easily be applied to Jerry. It was obvious though that Hannah thought he was wonderful so they were diplomatic in their answers. Linda was the first to speak. "Well, he's certainly different," she said hesitantly, "he's not what you'd describe as beautiful though."

Not knowing what else to say Linda turned to Moses for help. Moses sipped his tea and studied the bear carefully. He studied him from a distance and then up close peering deep into the bear's eyes. "He's certainly not beautiful in the conventional sense of the word," he said, "but his face is interesting."

By saying that Jerry was not beautiful in the conventional sense, Moses had been diplomatic in the extreme. Jerry looked like no other bear that either he or Linda had ever seen. The simple truth was that Jerry was horribly ugly. His mouth was twisted into a crooked grimace and where he may once have been furry there were now bare patches. Also, his eyes were looking in different directions, which gave the distinct impression that he was drunk. Moses studied the bear for a while longer then picked him up. Stroking the bear's threadbare head he said. "I would say that this bear has had a hard life and the best thing that could ever happen to him is to have someone like you to love and look after him Hannah." Satisfied with this opinion, she smiled happily.

Moses went with Hannah to the station and walked her down to the platform. He looked at her fondly as they stood waiting for the train; he had enjoyed his morning with her and was sorry she was going. "Come and see me again soon," he said.

"And Linda too?"

Moses smiled. "Yes, of course, and Linda too."

Hannah fell silent.

"Are you going to be in trouble when you get home?" Moses asked her.

Hannah nodded miserably.

Moses pointed to the box Jerry was in. "Is he worth it?"

"Yes, he's going to be my best friend."

"I'm sure he will be. And you've got to bring him with you when you visit me." As he spoke a train pulled into the station. The doors slid open and Hannah boarded. She stood by the doors and then suddenly said. "I'll tell you a secret Moses." The door mechanism hissed and as the doors closed Hannah shouted. "Jerry's alive, he really is." The doors slammed shut and the train moved away. Moses was startled, not so much by what Hannah had said but by the conviction in her voice and the earnest, desperate look on her face.

Hannah waved at Moses through the window. The train picked up speed and suddenly he was gone leaving Hannah staring out into the gloom with her jumbled, troubled thoughts. She sat down. There was bound to be a terrible row when she got home. Her father, she knew, would be furious. Twisting in her seat with anxiety she tried to think more positively. How would her father feel, for instance, when he saw the bear alive? He couldn't help but be impressed by that. And he would know she hadn't been making up stories. She quickly imagined how things would change. Her father would say sorry for not believing her, give her a cuddle and even be proud of her. She could so plainly see her family being amazed and delighted at the bear's antics. Thomas would bring his friends round and would be nice to her. And what a star she would be at school. The other girls would have to be friends with her when they saw Jerry. It would all be so wonderful, a new life where she was happy all the time. At that moment though, there was no escaping the fact that whatever she may have seen in the shop window the day before, the bear she now had in the box appeared to be nothing more than a very old and dirty ordinary teddy bear.

CHAPTER 8

"You spent fifty pounds on this?" Hannah's father was standing by the big table in the kitchen holding Jerry up by his ear.

"You're hurting him daddy," pleaded Hannah.

"Don't be so stupid," yelled her father. "It's not alive. It's nothing but a bundle of rags."

As Jerry had feared he would, Mr Watson banged him, face down, on the table. He had been carrying on in this fashion since Hannah had arrived home some twenty minutes ago and Jerry was getting pretty sick of it.

"He's an antique," said Hannah helplessly.

"No Hannah, it is not an antique, it is just an old and useless piece of rubbish. Dirty, filthy, useless, rubbish." And, as if to emphasise these last words, banged Jerry on the table again.

Jerry, as was usual on a Sunday morning, was suffering from a hangover. Not as bad as the one he'd had the previous morning, but on a scale of ten, easily an eight. He was lying face down on the kitchen table. Prince, the Watson family's pedigree red setter, sniffed him and growled menacingly baring a set of particularly vicious looking yellow teeth.

Jerry felt the dog's hot smelly breath on his face and decided that if he lived beyond today (and that was by no means certain) the dog would be number two on his hit list. Mr Watson was already a very firm number one.

Mrs Watson had initially been as angry as her husband and, of course, frantic with worry about Hannah's disappearance. But now she felt enough had been said and as her husband was about to launch into another tirade she cut in. "Okay George, Hannah knows she's done wrong and

I think that she's very sorry. She thought the bear was an antique and she thought you would be pleased." George looked at his wife and snorted. "Oh yes, today it's an antique. Yesterday she was telling us it was alive." He sat down and addressing his wife directly said. "She's nine years old and she sneaks off without a word to anyone. She chucks fifty quid away on a load of old rubbish and to cap it all she allows herself to be led off by some layabout street trash." His wife felt compelled to interrupt. "Hold on there just a minute George. I agree that Hannah shouldn't have done what she did but I don't think you're being fair to the Big Issue man. From what Hannah has said I think we ought to be grateful to him."

"Oh do you?" said Mr Watson. "Well I'm sure he does as well and he's probably waiting for us to go charging down there with a nice fat reward."

"That's a terrible thing to say," said Mrs Watson.

George ignored this and pushing the bear away from him in disgust muttered. "Some bloody antique. The girl's not right in the head."

Mrs Watson was beginning to lose her patience. She picked up the box. "Look, the bear is very old," she snapped, showing her husband the lid with the illustration depicting a cute looking bear with a guitar and a neat blue suit. Pointing to a line of writing on the side of the box she read out. "Copyright Pop Toys nineteen sixty five, it is nearly an antique. Now I don't know what Hannah was thinking about by doing what she did but it seems to me she cared what you thought."

"For God's sake Angela," said George grabbing the box, "it's not even the same bloody bear. If she actually had this bear," he said pointing at the picture on the box, "and it was in pristine condition and it still had its guitar and if she had the other three, it might have some value." He picked up Jerry from the kitchen table and giving him a good shake. "This bloody thing looks as if he would be more at home on a pub piano than playing a guitar." Shaking his head in disgust he threw Jerry into the utility room where he landed heavily on the tiled floor. Then turning to Hannah and wagging his finger he said. "You needn't think you're getting that thing back either. It's going in the rubbish and that's an end to it."

"But daddy," said Hannah.

"No buts," he said, pointing at Jerry sprawled on the floor. "Tomorrow that disgusting thing goes, and as for you young lady, up to your room now."

Knowing that there was no point in even thinking of arguing Hannah trooped up to her room in silence. She flopped onto her bed and stared miserably at the ceiling unable to make up her mind if she was more worried about her father's intention to get rid of Jerry or the awful fact that since she had had him, Jerry had shown absolutely no sign of life. Could it be that she had imagined what she had seen in the old shop window? Surely not. She had seen what she had seen. The bear had looked at her, walked past her and even stuck his tongue out. Had she got the wrong bear? Certainly not. there couldn't possibly be two bears that looked like this one. Sorrowfully Hannah concluded that she would probably never know now. Jerry was gone, her Christmas money was gone and she was in terrible trouble with her father.

The memory of walking to the old shop with Moses and how cosy it had been eating toast and drinking tea in Linda's shop and of being so happy meant nothing now. Alone in her room, Hannah could almost believe that all this had happened to someone else. It dawned on her that as well as losing Jerry she would also never see Moses and Linda again and that fact alone made her very sad. She couldn't hold back the tears any longer. They clouded her eyes and then spilt over and streamed down her cheeks and onto her pillow. She tried to choke back the sobs that welled up in her throat but couldn't. And in the end all she could do was lie on her bed and cry until eventually, miserable and exhausted, she fell into a deep dreamless sleep.

The next thing Hannah knew her mother was leaning over her shaking her gently, "Hannah darling, Hannah, wake up." She sat up and rubbed her sore and puffy eyes. Her mother smiled at her and gave her a hug. "Daddy wants to talk to you, he's downstairs in the sitting room."

Her mind, still sticky with sleep, she stared blankly up at her mother wondering what was going on and then after a couple of seconds the events of the morning came flooding back and a familiar heaviness descended on her heart. "Is he still very cross?" she asked.

Her mother gave her an encouraging smile. "Not as cross as he was," and taking Hannah's hand she led her downstairs.

In the sitting room Hannah's father was sitting, rather formally, in one of the big armchairs. His face was expressionless as he watched Hannah perch herself on the edge of the settee.

"Well young lady what have you got to say for yourself?" he asked sternly.

"Sorry daddy."

Mr Watson, his lips pursed and eyes locked on Hannah's, sat in silence for some time before saying. "You do know that mummy and I are very worried about you don't you?"

Hannah nodded meekly.

"And why do you think that is?"

Hannah hadn't been prepared for this and she had to think before she answered. "Because I went out and bought the teddy?"

Mr Watson nodded. "Well yes," he said slowly, "but it's not only that, there are other things as well." He leaned forward in his chair. "For a start your performance at school isn't very good is it?"

Hannah shook her head.

"You do know that it costs me an awful lot of money to send you to that school don't you Hannah?"

Hannah nodded solemnly.

"And it's not just the fees, it's the uniform and equipment and all the other little odds and ends to consider. Sending you to that school is a very expensive business."

Hannah felt wretched. She had fully expected to be told off for going off on her own this morning and she even accepted that she should be punished. And surely having to lose Jerry was a huge punishment. But if her father was now going to go on about her performance at school then that was simply unfair.

Hannah hated her school. She hated the loneliness of it and the sick feeling she got when the other girls laughed at her and whispered to each other.

Her father continued. "You do know that your school chum Tara is already looking to get into Oxford or Cambridge don't you? I was talking to her dad at the golf club a few days ago."

Hannah wanted to scream. Of course she knew all about Tara and her ambitions. Tara was the cleverest girl in the class and was always showing off and boasting. She was also the leader of the small gang of girls that bullied Hannah.

"If you want to be a success in life my girl," continued Mr Watson, "you have to think about these things. You have to take your opportunities. There's no time for daydreaming. I'm afraid the daydreamers of this world just get left behind and you don't want that do you?"

Hannah shook her head.

"You should bring Tara home here after school one day. She's the kind of friend that can get you on in life."

"But she's not my friend," said Hannah, "she's a bully and she calls me moose and she gets all the others to call me moose...."

Her father laughed, "but that's just a bit of harmless ribbing, life's rough and tumble. You really must toughen up Hannah."

There was no point in trying to get her father to see her point. This was one of his favourite topics. Hannah felt wretched and was just thinking that things couldn't possibly get any worse when he said. "Now, you remember Doctor Kingston whom you went to see last year when you had problems?"

Hannah's heart, already sinking, plummeted.

"Well I spoke to him on the phone this morning and he thinks that it might be a good idea if you went to see him again. Don't you think that would be a good idea too Hannah?"

Hannah knew that her father didn't care what she thought and that the decision had already been made. Aware that it was useless to argue she reluctantly nodded in agreement.

"Good," said Mr Watson, rubbing his hands together. "I'm glad we've sorted that out." He picked up his newspaper and taking a cigar from the box on the coffee table, sat back comfortably in his armchair.

Mrs Watson came into the room carrying a tea tray. She gave Hannah an encouraging smile and said brightly. "Have you two finished your chat?"

"We have," said her husband from behind his paper, "and Hannah agrees with me that seeing Doctor Kingston is a good idea."

"Have you told Hannah what Doctor Kingston said about the bear?" Mrs Watson busied herself pouring tea.

Her husband fidgeted awkwardly in his seat. "Oh yes, as if he had just remembered, "Doctor Kingston mentioned that as you bought that bear thing with your own money you should be allowed to keep it."

Hannah's heart leapt. This was the first bit of good news she had had since she got home. She didn't think though that it would look good to seem too cheerful, so for a while she kept a suitably gloomy expression on her face.

The thought of talking to the awful Doctor Kingston was too horrible to contemplate, but on this occasion at least he seemed to have done Hannah a good turn.

After a long silence Hannah asked. "Can I take Jerry up to my room?"

"You can have him later darling," said her mother, "he was filthy so I put him in the washing machine."

"Oh no," screamed Hannah. She jumped up from the settee and rushed out through the kitchen to the utility room. Jerry's sodden face, pressed against the glass door of the machine, stared out at her. Helplessly Hannah watched as the machine clicked on to the spin cycle.

CHAPTER 9

After Moses had seen Hannah off at the station he went back to Linda's shop to collect his magazines. Linda smiled at him as he walked in "What a sweet kid".

"Yeah," said Moses, "pity about the bear."

Linda laughed. "I still can't believe that she actually got it from that dreadful place. What did you think of it?"

"What, the bear?"

"No, the shop silly, what did you think of the shop?"

"Well I didn't go in," said Moses. "Hannah wanted to go in by herself so I just waited outside. Was it really a toy shop once?"

"Apparently, yes," said Linda, "but we're talking about a long time ago here, certainly before I was born."

"What, and the old guy, Old Jones, just decided to stop selling toys because he hated kids, is that it?"

"Well a bit of that maybe," said Linda. "That and other things; I remember telling my mum once that the old man was mad. I only said it because all the other kids said it.Anyway mum told me off for saying that. She said that he'd had a very tragic life. She told me that there had been some kind of incident back in the sixties, something to do with his wife and child."

"That's a shame," said Moses. "It's a bit of a mystery all this isn't it."

"Not really," said Linda. I guess the old guy just carries on. I suppose it's all he knows."

No, not that, Hannah's teddy bear. She said she saw it in the window yesterday, but when we got there, there was nothing to be seen. And when I pointed this out to her she said he was probably hiding."

"So what are you saying?"

Moses shook his head. "Nothing I guess, but have you ever seen anything in the window?

Linda shrugged."Nothing other than all those old advertising cards and stuff and they've been there forever."

Moses continued, "and then, just now as I was seeing her off at the station, Hannah said she has a secret and tells me that Jerry is alive.

The pair thought for a moment and then Linda spoke. "Hey Moses, I think it's pretty obvious that she is quite a lonely little girl. I reckon she saw the old shop yesterday, saw that it was once a toy shop and decided that it looked like a good place to buy a magic teddy bear. Little girls and their imagination."

Moses laughed at his own foolishness. Of course Linda was right.

He picked up his bundle of magazines and was about to leave, when Linda said. "Don't go yet, I've got a favour to ask. Her demeanour, perfectly relaxed before, suddenly became awkward. "Look I hope you don't mind me asking but I could really use someone to do a few odd jobs around here. I'll pay you of course," she said quickly, "if you've got the time that is."

"Sure thing," said Moses, "does any particular time suit you?"

Linda shrugged. "Whenever it suits you, I close at two-o-clock."

"Fine," said Moses. He left the shop and within a few minutes was busy selling his magazines. Steel-bright winter sunlight warmed the cold morning air. Moses inhaled it deeply. Life was suddenly good.

CHAPTER 10

It was three o'clock in the morning. Jerry was still sitting on the Aga stove where Hannah had put him after retrieving him from the washing machine. He had been gently steaming since six-o-clock and now, at last, he felt dry enough to move. Yesterday had been, without doubt, the worst day of his life and he had spent most of the night wondering what further outrages he would have to suffer while he was in this dreadful place. It was quite clear to Jerry that the whole family was insane and he was seriously worried about his future. On the face of things his plight looked pretty hopeless but he knew, no matter what, he had to get away from the house and back to the old shop. How he would achieve this escaped him for the moment, but given the urgency of the situation, he was sure he would think of something. That though he would think about later. Right now he had some scores to settle.

Prince was asleep in his basket but woke up and started a low growl when he saw Jerry climb down from the stove and make his way across the kitchen. He was still growling as Jerry dragged a chair across the kitchen, climbed on it and opened the fridge door, but when he caught sight of a joint of beef sitting temptingly on the lower shelf, the dog became silent and rousing himself from his basket slunk across the kitchen and joined Jerry by the open fridge.

"Oh, so Mr Smelly Breath wants to be friends now, does he?" Jerry leaned down, gave the dog a not too playful pat on the head and then tore off a chunk of meat and waved it under the dog's nose. As if pre-programmed, Prince sat and started to slobber uncontrollably. Jerry shook his head sadly. "What a dummy," he muttered and shoved the large chunks of tender flesh into the dog's mouth and watched as he wolfed it down. He then tore off another chunk of beef and threw it on the floor before turning his attention to feeding himself. He was starving.

The fridge was crammed full with all kinds of food, but more than the food Jerry noticed four cans of lager perched gloriously in the door shelf. A smile of pure joy suffused his ugly features. Falling to his knees and looking heavenward he said. "Oh thank you, thank you," and blew a grateful kiss as he gleefully yanked off a ring-pull.

Jerry swallowed the contents of the first can without pausing for breath and then let out a long jabbering burp of quite startling volume. After wiping his mouth on his sleeve he opened another can and took a few gulps from it. Feeling better than he had for a long time he then set about the joint, alternately cramming large chunks of tender flesh into his mouth and throwing scraps of fat at the dog, which accepted everything eagerly. When Jerry had eaten enough, he dragged the plate of meat out of the fridge and kicked it towards Prince who, hardly believing his luck, attacked it with gusto.

Jerry drank the rest of his lager and started frantically emptying the well-stocked fridge, throwing everything, as it came to hand, over his shoulder. Soon the kitchen floor was littered with cheese, butter, eggs, various packets of cooked meats, salad and sweets. Prince, standing in the centre of it all was sampling each new treat as it came his way. Finally, with some difficulty, Jerry dragged the substantial remains of a Black-Forest gateau off the top shelf. He ate a couple of generous mouthfuls himself and dumped the rest of it under the dog's nose. Prince momentarily looked up at Jerry before burying his face in the gooey cake. Clutching the two remaining beers Jerry climbed onto the work surface and settled himself in his place on the warm stove. Happily sipping his beer he watched the dog gorge itself.

Confused by the quantity and variety of food that surrounded him, Prince darted from one thing to another, treading everything into a squalid mess as he did so. After the gateau, Prince turned his attention to a wedge of cheese, which he bit in half. After that he swallowed, without bothering to chew, three thick slices of ham. Then he went back to the remains of the beef, which was now scattered all over the floor. He licked up a mush of broken eggs and milk and tore open a packet of bacon, shaking it violently as if he were killing a rat. But then the dog's pace started to slow and he began to struggle. He briefly licked up some more milk, but after this, gave up and tottered unsteadily back to his basket where he flopped down with a deep uneasy sigh. Jerry surveyed the scene happily.

It was about ten minutes later that Prince started a low pitiful whimpering. Jerry, who was just finishing off his last beer, watched with interest as the animal, which was obviously in some distress, stumbled from his basket and started pacing uneasily around the kitchen. The dog looked miserably up at Jerry, whining as he pawed the back door. Long streamers of dribble hung from his slack mouth.

Jerry gave him a friendly wave.

Shakily the dog circled the kitchen then stopped. His head hung forward and his body started to heave. His mouth opened and closed rhythmically as if he were trying to swallow a ball of air. Then he vomited. He cast a baleful glance in Jerry's direction and moved to another part of the kitchen where he vomited again, this time with a vengeance, producing a sticky beige pool that after spreading was as big as a dinner plate. The unhappy creature then staggered around whimpering and vomiting until there were at least half a dozen steaming pools scattered all around the floor. Jerry watched with fascination, hardly believing how much sick one animal could produce. "Well done," gasped Jerry with genuine admiration. This was better than Jerry could possibly have hoped for. The dog, now totally exhausted, collapsed into his basket. Jerry surveyed the scene of total devastation with a satisfied smile. The dog lolled in his basket looking up at Jerry with an expression that conveyed at the same time abject misery and undeniable guilt. Jerry grinned at him. "You're going to get a hiding for this lot you half-witted brute." He chucked his two empty beer cans in the direction of the dog basket and he threw back his head and laughed. He laughed until it hurt and even then he kept laughing and when he stopped laughing, drifted off into a semi-drunken, satisfied sleep.

At seven o'clock in the morning George Watson, freshly showered and dressed for the office, made his way down to the kitchen to make coffee. The house was still in darkness and it was from the hallway that, somewhat puzzled, he noticed the dim light from the open fridge door. He didn't though, until it was too late, notice the battlefield that the kitchen floor had become. His expensively shod foot skidded away from under him as he stepped in the pool of sick in the doorway. He fell heavily, managing as he did so to pitch forward and land squarely in the biggest puddle of sick and the leftover food that occupied the centre of the room. He twice tried to get up only to slip again on the slimy mess that surrounded him.

Hannah, along with the rest of the family, was woken by the sound of her father's furious voice and was soon standing in the kitchen doorway rubbing her sleepy eyes and gaping at the scene in front of her. Within seconds her mother and brother were alongside her.

"Oh gross," said Thomas.

Mr Watson was standing amid a scene of chaos shaking his fist and screaming at the dog, which was cowering in its basket. "You bloody greedy, stupid mutt."

"What on earth has happened George?" said Mrs Watson, hardly believing what she was looking at.

"Your damned dog," he shouted angrily turning on his wife. "Bloody thing opened the bloody fridge and ate all the bloody food."

"George, please don't shout and please don't use such awful language in front of the children."

He stared dumbly at her for a second, then shouted even louder. "For God's sake woman, I'm covered in bloody dog sick! What do you expect me to do? Pat the bloody thing on its bloody head and give it a bloody biscuit!"

White with frustrated rage, George stuck his tightly clenched fist under the terrified dog's nose. He was trembling with fury and for a while it seemed as if he might actually beat the dog up, but he resisted and instead turned his fury on his wife. "It's your wretched dog," he exploded "you can clear this lot up." And with that he stormed out of the kitchen and stomped noisily up the stairs, leaving behind him a trail of vomit.

Hannah's mother rolled her eyes, shook her head and followed her husband up the stairs. Thomas cast a final bleary-eyed glance at the floor and once again said. "Gross," before shuffling back up to his room.

Alone now Hannah stood in the doorway, gazing at the wasteland of the kitchen floor. She looked at Jerry perched on the Aga, not quite exactly as he had been the night before. Then something weird happened. As their eyes met, for the briefest moment, the bear's eyes appeared to focus on hers and the barest trace of a sinister smile flickered across his mouth. Hannah caught her breath and stepped back. She edged away from the kitchen holding the bear's gaze and, as she made her way up the stairs to her room, felt her heart pounding.

CHAPTER 11

After Hannah had left for school that morning Jerry enjoyed the simple pleasure of watching Mrs Watson clear up the mess in the kitchen. She roundly abused the dog while doing this, which Jerry thought was great fun. If he could have had a cigarette and a can of lager and maybe a chicken curry as well it would have been easily as good as his nights back at the old shop watching television. Once the mess was cleared up though Mrs Watson went out and Jerry soon became bored. With nothing else to occupy his mind he started to give some serious thought as to how he was going to get back to the old shop. Jerry didn't think that this would present too much of a problem. He would have to enlist the help of the girl, which would of course mean revealing the truth about himself. But that didn't matter as long as nobody else knew. The girl might tell her parents but they wouldn't believe her. Or she might refuse to take him back in which case he would embark on a policy of trouble making which, he knew, would eventually have her begging him to go. He doubted though if that would be necessary. The girl seemed pretty stupid and he was sure that with a combination of bullying and sweet-talking she could be made to do anything he wanted. He decided to act straight away. As soon as the girl got home from wherever it was that she had gone he would let her know all about himself. Looking on the bright side he thought that it might actually be quite fun. With a bit of luck he reckoned, he could be back at the old shop by the weekend.

When Hannah left school that afternoon, Tara, together with her two most obnoxious friends, Sylvia and Laura, were waiting outside the school gates. As she passed them they followed her and as usual started their mindless name-

59

calling. Hannah quickened her pace.

"What's your best subject Moose?" Laura asked, "being stupid?"

The other girls laughed loudly at this. Hannah walked faster and the girls started to trot to keep up with her.

"Bad luck for you they don't have exams in being backward, you'd pass easy," said Tara and then Sylvia chimed-in: "Or maybe you could get top marks for being half asleep." They all laughed again.

Hannah then broke into a sprint. The gang didn't bother trying to keep up with her. They just shouted a baying chorus of, "Moose! Moose! Moose!" until she was out of sight.

Normally, this incident, and the thought of having to endure similar treatment again tomorrow, would have been more than enough to send Hannah home feeling depressed and unhappy. But this afternoon was different; she had other things on her mind, so much so that Tara and her gang were forgotten almost immediately.

All day Hannah had been haunted by the look she had seen on the bear's face that morning. The bear was alive, she knew it, but for some reason he was choosing not to show it. What could that reason be, she thought, as she hurried home.

Thomas answered the front door. "Mum's out," he said in his usual listless monotone. He left Hannah to close the door and shuffled moodily down the hall muttering to himself about baby-sitting and then disappeared upstairs to his room. Hannah was never too pleased about being left at home with Thomas. He either ignored her or he became bossy and annoying. Today though she was happy for him to ignore her. There was a dull boom of heavy bass music coming from Thomas's room. This was Thomas playing along with his karaoke machine, which meant he was in trainee rock star mode, an activity that usually rendered him brain-dead. This suited Hannah perfectly.

Having no idea when her mother would return home, Hannah had to work quickly. She grabbed Jerry from the Aga and rushed upstairs with him whispering, "It's okay, I'm going to look after you properly from now on." She sat him on her desk by the window before returning hurriedly back down to the kitchen.

With Hannah out of the room Jerry allowed himself a sly knowing smirk. If he absolutely had to let the girl know about him he might as well make it memorable. He hopped down from the desk and looked around the room. It was very neat and tidy with shelves full of books and cheerful pictures showing sunny seaside scenes. Jerry had never been to the seaside; it looked like a nice place. He climbed onto Hannah's bed, which was unbelievably soft and jumped gently up and down enjoying its springiness, but soon got out of breath. Puffing slightly he sat down suddenly feeling very hungry and remembered he hadn't eaten since raiding the fridge and that had been in the early hours of the morning; it was evening now. He was also dying for a cigarette and a beer. He looked around him and concluded that this probably wasn't the kind of place where he would get either of those. Then he heard footsteps coming up the stairs and quickly jumping off the bed, scrambled back onto the desk.

Hannah came into the room carrying a tray laden with two glasses of milk, some biscuits and a jar of honey. Through lifeless eyes Jerry watched her as she bustled around laying everything out neatly on the desk. When everything was just as she wanted it Hannah sat at the desk facing Jerry. For a while she wondered what to do. She could only imagine that the process of getting the bear to do something would be like teaching an animal a trick. She would need to gain his trust which, she supposed, would take time and patience. Most of all she mustn't expect too much too soon.   He would, after all, be very nervous. "Slowly and gently," she whispered. Hannah made herself comfortable and then held up a glass of milk. Jerry's dull eyes stared at her blankly. She smiled at him and speaking very slowly and clearly as if she were addressing a foreigner or a half-wit said. "Do-you-like-milk?"

Hannah's behaviour confirmed what Jerry already thought – this child wasn't exactly bright. He watched as Hannah, beaming innocently, held the glass very close to his face and cooed in a tiny voice. "Wouldn't you like a nice glass of milk?" Picking up the jar of honey and waggling it under Jerry's nose she said. "Shall I put some nice honey in the milk?" and tilted the jar miming the action of pouring the honey into the glass of milk. "Shall I? Would you like that?" She moved a little closer smiling and nodding encouragingly. "Mmm, milk is very good for you."

Jerry picked his moment well. He thrust his face into Hannah's and barked. "Are you 'avin a laugh."

Scared out of her wits, Hannah pulled away from the bear toppling off her chair and landing flat on her back with the glass of milk spilt everywhere. Terrified she stared up at the bear which was leaning over the desk and looking down at her as she lay sprawled on the floor. His voice cracked into an ugly caricature of hers.

"Mmm, milk-is-very-good-for-you, would-the-little-bear-like-some? No I wouldn't," he shouted, "I'd rather stick a wasp up my furry butt than drink milk."

Hannah wanted to get up and run but was paralysed by fear. "For your information," said Jerry, "I hate milk and I hate honey, what I want is some real food and I want it now." He glared at Hannah and when she didn't answer, thrust his head forward belligerently and snapped. "Are you going to feed me?" Hannah couldn't speak. Furious, Jerry yelled at her. "What's the matter with you? Are you bleedin' stupid?" He jumped down from the desk and suddenly the iron grip of fear that had held Hannah was released. Mobile again, and fuelled by a combination of hysteria and blind terror, she scrambled frantically to her feet, flung herself across the room and through the bedroom door slamming it shut behind her. Gripping the door handle tightly holding the door closed, her heart pounded wildly. What on earth was that creature. Surely not a teddy bear? Was she dreaming? She certainly hoped so.

With Hannah out of the room Jerry stuffed all the biscuits in his mouth and then made himself comfortable on Hannah's bed. He had enjoyed that little episode immensely. He was quite sure after his performance that the girl would be more than happy to take him home, but right now Jerry needed food He waited a while and then called out gently. "Little girl."

Hannah didn't answer.

He called again, "I'm sorry if I scared you little girl. Why don't you come back in here?"

Her voice trembling, Hannah said, "What do you want?"

"I just want to talk to you," he said soothingly.

Hannah, still clinging grimly to the door, was aware that she couldn't stay where she was forever. Her hands were beginning to ache. She took a deep breath and slowly pushed the door open and cautiously peeped into her room.

The bear was sitting on her bed. He smiled at Hannah and patting the bed beside him said. "Come and sit down. We need to have a little chat." Hannah edged into the room and perched uneasily on the edge of the bed.

Still smiling Jerry spoke. "Now I'm really sorry if I

frightened you little girl but I think you should know one or two things about me."

Hannah was surprised that the bear's manner was now quite calm, almost friendly.

He continued. "Not only do I not like honey, as a general rule I tend to steer clear of anything that could be described as being of a healthy nature. This is because I don't consider 'healthy food' to be real food. Real food is pizza or curry or hamburgers and chips. Do you understand?" Hannah nodded.

"And as far as drink is concerned," said Jerry, his face cracking into a spiteful grin, "I feel happier sticking to things that have a fairly generous alcohol content rather than some horrible stuff that's been squeezed out of a cow's tits."

Hannah had listened to what the bear had just said but all she could think to say was. "Are you really alive?"

"I am at the moment," said Jerry, his voice heavy with impatience, "but that's a state of affairs that could change very soon if I don't get some food."

Flustered and slightly disturbed Hannah said, "What do you want?"

"Now we're talking," said Jerry happily, "now let me think. A pizza, or a curry, a really hot one." Hannah felt herself starting to panic again. She thought there might be some pizzas in the freezer but she wouldn't have a clue how to cook them. And, even if she did, her mother would be home soon and would wonder what on earth was going on if she came in to find Hannah trying to cook pizzas.

Suddenly Hannah's face brightened. "I know! Why don't you have some milk and biscuits for now and I'll bring you some of my dinner later on?"

Unable to contain his irritation any longer Jerry turned to Hannah and scowled fiercely. "I've already eaten the biscuits. I need real food. I'm starving."

His mood was turning ugly again. "Look, I'm getting pretty sick of this and, seeing as I never asked to be brought to this wretched hole, I think the very least you can do is make sure that I'm looked after. So if you don't mind, will you please sort me out a pizza and a couple of cans of lager and while you're at it you can bring me some cigarettes."

Suffering from what was becoming a state of permanent hysteria Hannah stared at the bear for a few seconds before spluttering lamely. "I don't know how to cook."

Jerry gave her a withering look. "You don't have to do any cooking you dummy. You just phone up and some bloke on a motorbike brings it. That's what Old Jones does. And after I've eaten you and me need to talk, there are certain things, important things, that we need to sort out."

Totally out of her depth now Hannah was close to melt down. Her mother would go mad if she ordered a takeaway, but she was also worried what the bear would do if she didn't feed him. She couldn't stand another outburst like the one earlier.

Suddenly Hannah heard Thomas come clumping along the landing. He stuck his head round her door and looked around the room. Hannah looked anxiously at Jerry who, she was amazed to see, had now become his former lifeless self. Thomas looked at the bear sitting on the bed next to Hannah and grinned maliciously. "Oh how sweet, Hannah and her little teddy having a cosy chat."

"Go away," said Hannah.

Thomas ignored her and in a flash he was across the room and grabbed Jerry from the bed.

"The famous dancing bear becomes the famous flying bear," he said, swinging Jerry around by his leg. Hannah jumped up and tried to rescue Jerry but Thomas pushed her away. Laughing, he swung the helpless bear around a few more times and then pitched him across the room. Jerry dropped neatly into the wastepaper basket.

"Slam dunk," shouted Thomas punching the air and he went back to his room still laughing loudly.

Hannah pulled Jerry out of the basket and sat him back on her bed, apologising to him as she did so. But Jerry, furious and badly shaken, simply stayed motionless and mute propped up against a pillow. Hannah tried to explain that Thomas hadn't meant any harm but Jerry remained resolutely lifeless. After a while Hannah gave up and disappointed, but relieved that at least that the bear had stopped his impossible demands, she mopped up the spilt milk and cleared away the tea things. "I'll bring you some food up later," she said as she left the room. Jerry sulked silently on the bed and added Thomas's name to his hit list.

It was bedtime when Jerry decided to talk again and this was only because Hannah had managed to smuggle some leftovers from dinner up to her room and by now he was too hungry to sulk any longer. The tray she was carrying was covered with a table napkin.

"Is it pizza?" said Jerry, scrambling down from the bed.

"Sort of, but much better." Hannah tried to sound convincing as she set the tray down on the desk. Jerry climbed eagerly onto the chair as she threw back the cloth revealing the food.

He surveyed the spread without enthusiasm. "What is it?" he asked suspiciously.

"Vegetarian quiche with brown rice. Mummy cooked it."

Jerry picked up the wedge of quiche, sniffed it and then studied it from all angles. Hannah smiled at him encouragingly. He took a bite.

"Nice?" said Hannah hopefully.

The bear rolled the quiche around his mouth cautiously. The immediate sensation was of something without flavour, which was at the same time was both slimily soggy and crustily dry. Too hungry not to eat, Jerry chewed it unhappily.

"Don't you like it?" said Hannah.

"No," said Jerry when he had eventually managed to swallow a mouthful.

"Why not?"

"Because it's bloody horrible," he said bluntly. "It tastes like a wet carpet tile." He took another bite, much larger this time, and shovelled some rice into his mouth screwing his face into a grimace of disgust as he chewed.

"Why are you eating it if you don't like it?"

"Because eating this crap is marginally better than dying of starvation," said Jerry. He continued eating until the plate was empty, licked it clean and dumped it on the bed. "Did you get me some booze and some fags?"

"Of course not!" said Hannah, shocked that he should even ask.

The bear rolled his eyes. "Surprise, sur-bleedin'-prise. So what the bleedin' hell are we supposed to do now then?"

"You know you really shouldn't swear so much," said Hannah.

"Why not?"

"Because they're bad words".

"Well maybe if I wasn't having such a bad time I wouldn't use such bad words," said Jerry. "I've got nothing to do. There's not even a bleedin' TV to watch."

"Well we can talk," said Hannah.

"Oh yeah, what about?"

"I don't know. It was you who said we had to talk. Don't you remember? When Thomas came in the room."

Jerry's face darkened. "Oh yeah, is your brother always like that?"

Hannah nodded. "He shows off a lot. He's always acting big and clever." She thought for a while and then said. "Why did you pretend to not be alive in front of Thomas?"

"Because it suited me," said Jerry grumpily, "You know about me but no one else needs to."

"Can't I tell mummy and daddy?"

"I thought you already had," said Jerry.

"Yes I did," said Hannah, "but they didn't believe me. They will though, if they see you like this."

"Yeah well you can forget that 'cos it ain't gonna happen."

Jerry knew he really should start working on getting Hannah to take him back to the old shop but he'd had a long day. And now, miserable at the prospect of facing the evening without a drink or a smoke, he really didn't feel he could cope with the barrage of stupid questions that he knew Hannah would launch at him. She might start crying too and he certainly couldn't put up with that.

"Are you sure you can't get me a couple of cans of lager and some fags?" he asked hopefully.

"I can't," said Hannah. "Mummy and daddy would kill me and I'm in awful trouble already."

"Right, then I'm going to get some kip" and with that he curled up on the end of Hannah's bed and promptly fell asleep.

CHAPTER 12

It was the middle of the night and for some reason Hannah woke up. She turned on her bedside lamp and was alarmed to see that Jerry had gone. Fearing what he might be up to she scrambled out of bed and went off in search of him. She found him downstairs in the sitting room on the big settee. He was holding a glass of brandy and a large cigar. Both looked enormous in his small paws, but he seemed to be managing them quite well. "What are you doing?" whispered Hannah, "it's not morning yet."

"Well, I was trying to get a bit of peace and quiet," said Jerry.

She sat down beside him. "You know you shouldn't really be doing that," she said, pointing to the cigar Jerry was smoking, "it's very bad for you."

"What like vegetarian quiche?"

"No, that's good for you."

"Well how come that made me feel sick and this doesn't?"

Hannah didn't know the answer to this so she ignored it and asked something she'd been dying to ask him since she'd first seen him in the old shop window. "Is it magic you being alive?"

Jerry looked keenly at her, his head cocked on one side. "How old are you?"

"Nine".

"What and you still believe in magic?"

"Well, not really," said Hannah feeling foolish, "but you are a bit like magic aren't you, you know, with being alive and everything. How did it happen?"

"I got bored," said Jerry.

"What so you came to life?"

"Well I didn't have a lot of choice did I?" I was stuck in

that bleedin' shop window for gawd knows how long with sod all to do."

"Oh," said Hannah disappointed. "And that's it?"

"That's it," said Jerry. "What did you expect, the fairy queen sprinkling stardust on me?"

Still feeling this explanation to be unsatisfactory Hannah said. "Well it must be a little bit like magic. After all you are alive aren't you?"

"Well that depends very much on your definition of living," said Jerry, "I don't think being stuck here with you can be called living. This must be the most boring place in the world."

"Well it needn't be," said Hannah. "We can be friends, we can do things together."

"Like what?"

Hannah tried desperately to think of something that Jerry might enjoy. "We could go out and play in the garden, there's a swing out there."

"Oh whoopeedoo," said Jerry. "Will the fun never end?"

"Well what do you want to do then?" said Hannah helplessly.

"Well right at this minute," said Jerry, "I want to have a smoke and get wrecked without being bothered by an annoying little tick who's life is so sad that she needs to believe in magic." He took a large swallow of brandy and puffed on his cigar.

Hurt and humiliated, Hannah retorted. "Well if you're going to be horrible I'm going to bed and you can sit down here on your own."

"Well don't let me stop you," said Jerry.

"And you'd better not leave all this stuff lying around," Hannah said, pointing to the bottle of brandy and the ashtray.

Jerry turned to her, gave her a reassuring smile and said soothingly. "Don't worry little girl, I'll clear it all away. No one will ever know I was here."

Hannah paused in the doorway. "When I was at the old shop I wished for a best friend. I thought it might be you."

"Fat chance of that," chuckled Jerry as Hannah trailed miserably up the stairs back to bed.

By the time Jerry decided to go to bed he was so drunk that more than once he nearly fell over. He was carrying a tray. It had on it a considerably depleted bottle of brandy, a glass and an ashtray which contained the remains of the two cigars. The large tray and its contents were awkward for him to carry and he was further hampered by the regular need to smother sudden bursts of drunken giggling.

CHAPTER 13

For the second morning running Hannah was woken by the sound of angry voices. This morning though it was her mother and Thomas who were doing the shouting. She was very relieved to see Jerry curled up on the end of her bed.

"I don't know, someone must have put them there." Thomas's voice carried that whiney edge it always had when he was being told off.

Keen to know what was going on, Hannah sidled across the hall and stood alongside her mother in Thomas's doorway. He was sitting up in bed and beside him on the floor was a nearly empty bottle of brandy, an empty glass and an ashtray containing the remains of two cigars. "I don't know I tell you. Honestly I don't."

Seeing Hannah, Thomas turned on her and demanded, "did you put these here?"

"Oh for God's sake Thomas!" said Mrs Watson angrily, "she's just a child. I hardly think she could manage two cigars."

They were soon joined by Mr Watson who had been in the bathroom. He strode purposefully down the hall his face covered in shaving cream. "What's all the noise about?" he said impatiently.

Mrs Watson turned away from Thomas in disgust. "See for yourself. I came in to wake him up and this is what I found."

He put his head round the door and looked at the damning evidence by Thomas's bed. "There's nothing big and clever about this you know," he said sternly.

Thomas gave an anguished howl. "But it's nothing to do with me."

"Well who is it to do with then?" demanded his father. "I suppose this is all part of being a rock star is it?"

"I can't believe this," groaned Thomas.

"Oh can't you," said Mr Watson, "well there are a few things I can't believe either. For a start I can't believe that the dog opened the fridge and helped himself to a couple of cans of lager, so I think the other night's little mystery has been solved."

"What!" said Thomas. "You're blaming me for that?"

Well I can't see any reason why I shouldn't, can you? I think you've got a bit of a problem young man."

"This is so unfair," wailed Thomas.

"Well if all this rock and roll business makes you behave like a degenerate then I think there had better be a few changes around here." He pointed at the karaoke machine. "You can damn well do without that for a while".

"You can't do that," Thomas protested.

"Oh yes I can and there's a few other things I can do, starting with grounding you for a month and stopping your pocket money."

With this his father barged into the room, picked up the karaoke machine and dumped it on the landing. Then, standing by Thomas's bed with arms folded, he said. "Now I want the truth. Is this it, or is there more?"

"What are you talking about?" said Thomas genuinely puzzled.

"Drugs my lad, that's what I'm talking about – puff, dope, weed."

Thomas pulled his duvet over his head and groaned again.

Hannah went back to her bedroom, closing the door behind her. Jerry was still asleep. She gave him a sharp prod and a flicker of life crossed his face. "Jerry," she hissed, "Thomas is in terrible trouble with daddy."

"Good," said Jerry, "serves the little git right."

"Did you put that stuff by his bed?"

"Of course I did".

"But why?"

"Because he swung me round his head and threw me in the rubbish bin."

"Yes, but now he's being told off for something he didn't do."

Jerry gave a contemptuous snort. "How wonderful, and just when I was beginning to think that God was on holiday."

Despairingly Hannah said. "But you don't understand, daddy is ever so cross with him. He's making him stay in for a whole month and he's stopped his pocket money."

"Well tough titty," said Jerry.

"But Thomas is really upset."

"Well if it bothers you so much why don't you tell them the truth?" snapped Jerry. "Go on, tell them I did it. And while you're at it let them all carry on pushing you around." He sat up. "You must be the world's number one mug. You get pushed around by everyone and then beg for more. Why don't you get angry? Everyone needs a bit of the nasty git in them. You want to be a bit more like your old man. He's got plenty of the nasty git in him. Not as much as me but more than enough to get by."

Hannah got the gist of what Jerry was saying but decided not to carry the conversation any further, partly because she needed to get ready for school but partly, also, because deep inside she knew that there was more than a little truth in what Jerry had said.

Hannah went down to breakfast and placing Jerry on the Aga, joined Thomas at the kitchen table. Normally Thomas would have had plenty to say about both Jerry and Hannah but this morning she noticed, with a certain amount of pleasure, he was unusually quiet.

Once breakfast was over, one by one Mr Watson,

Thomas and Hannah left the house. Jerry, nursing another hangover, sat listlessly on the Aga watching Mrs Watson tidy the kitchen. Jerry had not forgotten that it was this woman who had put him in the washing machine and so he viewed her as a very dangerous person indeed. He kept a wary eye on her as she bustled around the kitchen and suffered a moment of high anxiety when, from the utility room, he heard the dreaded washing machine whir into life. It soon became clear though that for today, at least, she had no intention of washing him.

At about eleven-o-clock Mrs Watson went out. Jerry waited for a while and, when he felt fairly certain that she wasn't immediately coming back, jumped down from the Aga and did some exploring. First he went into the drawing room and taking another bottle of brandy from the drinks-cabinet, drank quite a lot of it. Feeling much better he went out to the utility room where he stared with a curious mixture of fear and fascination at the gurgling, rumbling washing machine. Then he squeezed himself into the narrow gap behind the machine where he found an interesting selection of pipes and rubber hoses.

At school Hannah couldn't concentrate on anything. She was bursting with excitement and dearly wished she had a friend to share her secret with. For now it didn't matter that Jerry was so awful. She just wanted to tell someone about him. A few of her classmates were quite nice to her at times but, whenever they looked like they were going to be real friends with her, Tara and her gang would find a way of spoiling things. What Hannah really wanted was Jerry to be her friend, but he didn't seem to want to be friends with anyone, least of all her.

It was as they were about to go home that Miss Mason, the form mistress, called the class to attention. She tapped her desk with a ruler and the class fell silent.

"On Friday," she announced, "we are going to have a history exam. So for your homework tonight I want you to do revision. Now to do that you will need to take home your history books so you can study what we have covered this term. And you will also need your revision books to make notes in. Do you all understand that?" The girls nodded. "Now, it is very, very important that you bring both of these books into school tomorrow, because, in my infinite generosity," she smiled at the girls and was rewarded with a ripple of laughter, "I have decided to let you have even more revision time tomorrow afternoon so that you will all have the best possible chance of doing well in the exam." Miss Mason then became very serious. "Now I don't think I have to tell you that I will not be pleased if anyone comes to me and says they've left their books at home." She looked from face to face and when satisfied this final message had sunk in, said brightly. "Okay girls off you go," and with that the class was dismissed.

As Hannah filed out of school she checked her bag to make sure the books were there. Then she made a decision. Tonight, as soon as she had done her homework, she would do her best to make Jerry her friend.

Considering that the past few days had consisted of little else, Hannah should not have been surprised upon returning home from school to find her mother dealing with yet another disaster. The kitchen floor was flooded and Mrs Watson, wearing a posh dress and green Wellington boots, was furiously mopping the floor. "What happened?" said Hannah.

"The washing machine, it's gone wrong."

"Do you want me to help you?"

"No," said her mother quite firmly. Then sighing deeply

said. "It's okay. I'm not cross with you I'm just a bit stressed that's all. Daddy and I are supposed to be going to the theatre tonight and quite honestly I could have done without this." Mrs Watson looked at her watch. "God, he'll be home any minute." Then she smiled at Hannah. "You go and do your homework. This won't take me long." She gave a little laugh." At least the floor will be nice and clean." Hannah was about to go when her mother called her. Paddling across the wet floor she picked Jerry up from the Aga. "Will you take him upstairs with you sweetheart. Every time I see him he makes me jump. I keep thinking someone's watching me," she said, handing the bear to Hannah, "if I didn't know better I'd think that your little friend here was responsible for all this."

"Why?" Hannah asked anxiously.

"No reason," her mother said, surprised at Hannah's reaction. "I was only joking darling. Don't worry I'm not going to throw him away."

"Okay mummy," said Hannah taking Jerry from her.

Her mother laughed. "I think the best thing you two can do is to go to your room and get on with your homework."

Hannah climbed the stairs to her room. "You did that didn't you?"

Jerry hung lifelessly in Hannah's arms. "I know you can hear me," she said as she sat him on her bed and gave him a shake. Jerry didn't respond. Determined not to let him get away with ignoring her, Hannah thought for a while and then started inspecting him closely, looking behind his ears and at his neck, "I think you could do with a wash. I'd better take you down to mummy."

She felt him wriggle. Pleased with her cunning Hannah sat Jerry on the bed. He glared at her. "That's not fair."

"No, and nor is messing up the kitchen. Poor mummy has

got to clean it all up now."

"Well she shouldn't have tried to kill me in that washing machine thing."

"She didn't try to kill you. She just wanted you to be nice and clean. Why do you have to be so horrible?"

"Because that's the way I am," said Jerry and, seeing an opportunity continued, "if you don't like it, why don't you take me back to the old shop and get a refund?"

Hannah hadn't expected this and it was a little while before she spoke. "Do you want to go back to the shop?"

Jerry was just about to answer but as he opened his mouth Mr Watson put his head around the door. He didn't look at all happy. He glanced distastefully at Jerry who, once again, in the blink of an eye, had assumed his lifeless pose.

"Who were you talking to Hannah?"

"I was playing," said Hannah slightly embarrassed.

"I thought you were supposed to be doing your homework,"

"I was just going to," she said.

"Yes, well it would be a good idea if you got on with it instead of playing silly games with that thing. Now listen," he continued. "Mummy and I are going to the theatre this evening, and what with all this washing machine nonsense, she hasn't had time to prepare a meal, so I've left some money downstairs. Thomas can order a takeaway." Looking at his watch he said. "We really must hurry. Be good." He gave Jerry another look as he left the room. "You know you really shouldn't be playing with toy bears at your age Hannah."

CHAPTER 14

Jerry had intended spending the evening bullying Hannah into taking him back to the old shop but when the pizza arrived, piping hot and smothered with pepperoni and chilli peppers, it proved to be too much of a distraction. He sat on the end of Hannah's bed chomping away happily and she couldn't help noticing that in Jerry's case a full stomach certainly sweetened his temper. After his fifth slice Jerry became positively chatty and seemed to be almost enjoying telling her about his life at the old shop.

"Are any other toys alive?" asked Hannah.

"Of course they are. All toys are alive."

"What, even my toys in this room?"

The bear nodded, his mouth full of pizza.

Hannah looked around the room. "Well why aren't they talking to us?"

"Because they can't, they're only toys."

Feeling this statement contradicted all that Jerry had said before she said. "But you just said they're alive."

"Well yes, they are, but not like you and me. They've no need to be, have they?"

Hannah was beginning to get confused. "Haven't they?"

"Of course not. They're bought toys so they were given a life."

"Is that how it works? You have to buy a toy to give it a life?"

"Well there's no other way is there?" said Jerry almost as if Hannah was stupid to ask. "When a kid gets a toy the toy gets a life. Simple."

Hannah thought about this for a while. "Well what about you? You were alive before I bought you. I saw you in the shop window."

"Yeah, well I didn't have much choice did I? No one was going to give me a life so I had to make one for myself." Jerry said this while stuffing the last slice of pizza in his mouth. Hannah had the vague feeling that what Jerry had just said contained some universal truth. And that if she could just grasp this truth she would be better able to cope with her own life. She studied the bear keenly wondering if he possessed a deep wisdom that she was failing to understand. But watching him eat with his mouth open and tomato sauce smeared down the side of his face, concluded that this probably wasn't the case. She had never seen anyone over the age of three eat so messily.

"How old are you?"

Jerry stopped chewing and thought for a while. "I don't know. How old are the Beatles and the Rolling Stones?"

"The Rolling Stones!" gasped Hannah. "They're ancient. My dad likes them. He likes the Beatles too but they aren't even a band anymore."

Jerry, chomping noisily as he spoke, said. "Yeah, well however old they are that's how old I am."

Hannah could hardly believe Jerry was that old.

"So you've been living at the old shop all that time without anyone knowing about you? And no one has ever seen you?"

"Well of course a few people have seen me," said Jerry, "I got caught out a couple of times." He slurped some cola and grimaced. Looking at the can with distaste. "You know I really would have preferred a beer. This stuff can't be good for you."

Hannah ignored this. "Who saw you?" she asked excitedly.

Jerry shrugged. "Just people, passers by."

"But why didn't they buy you like I did."

"Because they weren't so bleedin' stupid,"

"Well why didn't they go in the shop and tell the old man what they'd seen?"

"I dunno, maybe some did."

"Why didn't he do anything?"

"Well I suppose he wouldn't have believed them. Why should he?"

"He believed me," said Hannah.

"Yeah? My-furry-butt he did," said Jerry scornfully, "all he believed was that you had fifty quid and were stupid enough to give it to him."

Hannah had made a decision to ignore any hurtful remarks Jerry might make and concentrate on being positive. So when he said this she simply sipped her fruit-juice and waited before speaking again.

"Well I think you must be very clever to have lived in the shop for all that time without Mr Jones seeing you".

Jerry laughed. "Do you actually think that the old boy hasn't seen me? Do me a favour. He's seen me quite a few times but thankfully only when he's drunk."

"What, and that's okay?"

"Well it's okay in one way. He never has a clue what's going on when he's had a skin full, but the downside is that he tends to lay off the booze for a bit which don't suit me, 'cos when he's not havin' a booze, I don't get a drink. He saw me dancing on the counter one night."

"Really?" gasped Hannah. "What did he do?"

"Packed up drinking for a fortnight".

The image Hannah had in her head of Jerry dancing made her smile. "Why were you dancing on the counter?"

"'Cos' that's what I do. I'm Jerry the 'Rock and Roll Teddy Bear'. Lead singer of The Jericho's. There was some Rhythm and Blues blaring out of the radio so I was giving it the old air guitar." Jerry mimed playing the guitar and did a curious little hopping dance.

Hannah giggled. "Oh do it again Jerry, please, do the whole thing."

"You're 'avin a laugh aren't you?" said the bear. "No music, no can do and anyway it would knacker me."

"Oh please Jerry, sing a song for me, please." Hannah had a sudden thought. "You can use Thomas's karaoke machine, it's on the landing and daddy has still got the tapes for the machine. Oh please Jerry, please."

"Forget it, I'm too old for all that." He settled back down on the bed and folded his arms stubbornly across his chest.

Hannah sat on the bed next to him. Then slyly turned to him and said, "I'll get some beer and cigarettes for you."

Jerry considered this proposition for maybe two seconds before saying. "Okay."

Delighted, as much with her own cunning as with the prospect of seeing Jerry perform, Hannah scurried downstairs and after taking two cans of beer from the fridge went into the sitting room and took a handful of cigarettes from the case on the coffee table and the box of karaoke tapes from her father's bureau. Thomas, she was pleased to note, was well out of the way, conveniently watching a noisy football match in the TV room.

Back in her room Hannah placed the goodies on her bed. Jerry seized one of the cans and drank the beer down greedily. Then he lit a cigarette and started to rake through the box of tapes.

"There's some good stuff here," he said with grudging admiration.

Hannah busied herself dragging the karaoke machine in from the landing and clearing her desk so that Jerry could use it as a stage. When she had set everything up she added a final touch by bending the flexible stem of her desk lamp so it would shine upwards like a stage light. She then turned to Jerry. "Is that okay?"

Jerry handed her a tape "It'll need to be loud," was all he said as he clambered up onto the desk. Hannah turned the main bedroom light out, leaving Jerry illuminated by the soft glow of the desk light.

"Ready?" she asked as she stood with her finger poised over the play button.

He nodded and the room was instantly filled with a menacing blues guitar rift. Jerry immediately started strutting around the makeshift stage. Delighted, Hannah clapped along with the beat. As the introduction played him in, Jerry thrust the microphone close to his mouth and started to sing. His raw growling voice was perfectly suited to the anarchic lyrics and, as he sang, his face took on a demonic stare. Hannah watched him breathless with excitement as he stomped around. Jerry was a natural performer, fizzing with energy and belting out the song like a true rock star. And when the final chorus was over, he threw his arms up in the air to acknowledge the applause of a vast imaginary audience. Hannah jumped up clapping and cheering. He bowed to Hannah and then turned to the left and right bowing extravagantly. He faced the window and was about to bow again but froze. A rubbish truck, its amber warning light flashing, was trundling down the road towards the house. Terrified, the bear scrambled down from the desk and dived under the bed. Hannah, still buzzing with excitement from the show, didn't understand what was going on.

"What on earth is the matter?" she asked peering under the bed.

"Has it stopped?" whispered Jerry.

"Has what stopped?"

"The rubbish truck, has it stopped outside?"

Hannah went to the window and watched the truck pass. "No," she said, "it's gone."

Jerry crawled out from under the bed and with trembling paws opened the second can of beer. He took a few breathless gulps.

"What's the matter," said Hannah anxiously. "Why should the rubbish truck stop here?"

Slightly calmer, but with eyes still wild, Jerry said. "To get me."

CHAPTER 15

It was Tuesday evening and Moses had just finished putting up some shelving in Linda's shop, the last of the numerous jobs that she had asked him to do. Linda had ordered a Chinese meal and now, with the various dishes all laid out, they were ready to eat. "I hope you're hungry," she said handing him a set of chopsticks, "I seem to have slightly over ordered." Dipping a prawn ball into a pot of sauce she said. "Those shelves look great" and continuing almost casually, "I've got you a job."

Busy manipulating his chopsticks in a dish of noodles Moses spoke without looking up. "I thought the shelves were the last thing on the list."

"No, not an odd job, a real job."

He looked up sharply. "What kind of a job?"

"Does it matter? The other day when we were talking you said you wanted a job, any kind of job would do you said. You meant that didn't you?"

Moses, who was now looking directly at Linda his chopsticks poised in mid air said. "Yes, yes I did."

"Well I got you one," Linda said simply.

"Am I allowed to ask what kind of job it is?"

"Dirty and cold with low pay and unsociable hours. Well that's according to Mikey, but I think he was trying to dress it up," said Linda.

"Sounds great," said Moses, "who's Mikey?"

"He's my big brother and, if you decide to take this wonderful opportunity, he'll be your boss."

Moses spooned some fried rice onto his plate. "And so how did all this happen?"

"By accident really," said Linda, taking a sip of her fruit juice, "I was at mum and dad's and Mikey was there and I was talking about you and he happened to mention he was short of guys on the late shift."

"And?" said Moses.

"And he asked when you can start."

"So when can I start?"

Linda laughed. "Are you serious? Don't you want to know more?"

Moses's face cracked into a grin. "Well I suppose I'll need to know where I need to go to do this job, but apart from that"....he shook his head, "if you've taken the trouble to find me a job that is not only cold and dirty but also low paid, then I think I can wait to find out what the downside is." He shrugged, "I'll do it."

"You sweet guy," said Linda, "and here was me thinking you were going to go all macho on me and say, 'I don't need no woman to find me a job'."

Moses laughed." Well, I might have got upset if you'd found me a good job. But this one sounds awful enough for me not to feel too indebted to you" and tucking into his noodles said, "is your brother as bossy as you?"

CHAPTER 16

Hannah emptied the contents of her school bag onto the floor in her bedroom and transferred everything into her large sports bag, taking extra care not to forget the two history books Miss Mason had spoken about the previous afternoon. She looked at Jerry, asleep and sprawled awkwardly in the small bed that she had made up for him. Then she went to the bathroom and returned a few moments later with a wet face cloth and a towel. She allowed herself a brief sly grin and, before he had time to know what was happening, pinned him down firmly and washed his face until it was thoroughly clean and without a trace of last night's pizza.

"What did you do that for?" spluttered Jerry angrily when she had finished.

"Because you were dirty." She then picked him up and put him in her bag, zipping it up quickly. She let him struggle and kick for a while and then, unzipping the bag just enough to show his furious face, said. "If you don't keep quiet, I'll tell mummy you need washing and then she'll put you in the washing machine" and zipped the bag shut again.

"Why have you put me in here?" Jerry's muffled voice moaned from inside the bag.

"Because you're coming to school with me," said Hannah surprisingly firmly.

"But why?" he wailed.

"Because Mummy and I are supposed to be going Christmas shopping tonight and I don't want to miss out on that because you've burned the house down." She picked up the bag. "Now shut up."

At school, peeking out of Hannah's bag tucked under her desk, Jerry spent the first part of the morning sulking. At

89

break time, while the classroom was empty, he grudgingly ate a Mars bar Hannah had left him. Jerry liked Mars bars and by the time the girls filed back into the classroom he was feeling better. The large sports bag was quite comfortable and even through the forest of desk and chair legs he had a good view of what was going on. There was a lot of activity with pots of paint and coloured pencils which looked like good fun. Jerry almost wished he could join in.

Just before the lunch break after everything had been cleared away, Miss Mason addressed the girls. Jerry was amazed how quickly she could get them to be quiet. His own experience of children when they used to come into Old Jones's shop was that they were noisy and unruly and would only respond to threats of physical violence. This woman however only had to place her fingers to her lips and there was almost immediate silence. Jerry was impressed.

"Now listen carefully girls," she said. "As you all know, when we come back after lunch we are going to spend the afternoon revising for Friday's history examination". The class listened intently. "I have been busy preparing the exam papers over the past two weeks and I now have everything ready to print". She held up a CD. "All the questions are on this disk and they all relate to things that we have studied throughout the term. So if you revise properly it will be as good as seeing what is on this CD." She looked around the class. "Has everyone remembered their homework and revision books?" There were a few murmured yeses and some nods. "All right then class," said Miss Mason brightly, "I look forward to seeing you all after lunch."

With all the girls at lunch Jerry was having a sleep in the quiet classroom. He woke up when the door opened and three girls came in. They were all giggling excitedly. One of the girls whispered. "Stand by the door Sylvia and keep a look out." Then, to his astonishment, the two others girls came over to where he was, and kneeling down by Hannah's bag, pulled him out and threw him roughly on the floor. They then hurriedly went through Hannah's belongings, rummaging around until they triumphantly pulled out two books. "I can't wait to see that little loser's face when she can't find these," said one, as both girls stifled fits of hysterical laughter. Jerry watched as one of the girls put the books into her own bag and zipped it up. While she did this, the other girl put the rest of Hannah's belongings very neatly back into her bag. The last thing she put back was Jerry himself. She turned to her friends and holding him up giggled. "Moose's monster." This caused them both to burst into a fit of smothered laughter again. Still giggling, they stuffed Jerry roughly back into the bag and quickly left the room.

When the class reassembled, Miss Mason told all the girls what she expected of them. "I want you all to work very quietly and go through your revision books and study what we have been discussing and learning this term. I'm going to be very busy preparing your exam papers, so I don't want any interruptions. I will remind you once again that revision for an exam is something you do by yourself. You don't need to ask me anything." She stood silent for a while and when she was happy they all understood what she had been saying, said. "Could you now please all get your books out."

There was a flurry of activity and a soft murmuring as bags and satchels were undone and books, pens, pencils and various other useful items were produced and placed on desks.

As the room returned to its former stillness it was Hannah alone who was left searching through her bag. Her hands burrowed through the contents. She pushed Jerry to one side and dug deeply into the bag, turning over anything that might possibly be concealing the precious history books. Slowly it dawned on Hannah that her search was useless, the books weren't there. Panic gripped her. How could she have forgotten them? Tears of frustration filled her eyes and the silence of the room weighed like lead on her heart as she hopelessly churned through the contents of the bag.

Miss Mason's voice cut through the silent room. "Hannah Watson. Could you please bring your books to me."

Hannah felt hot and knew her face must be very red. She looked at Miss Mason who was now standing behind her desk. "Now please Hannah." The teacher held her hand out.

Too tired and dispirited to search anymore Hannah said meekly. "I can't find them Miss."

The classroom fell silent. "Stand up please Hannah."

Hannah stood and for a moment caught the eye of Tara sitting at the desk directly in front of her. She smirked maliciously.

"What do you mean you can't find them Hannah?" said Miss Mason.

"I put them in my bag this morning Miss, but now they're not there."

"Well where are they?"

"I don't know, they must have got lost."

At this point Miss Mason erupted. "If they were in your bag how could they have got lost?" she demanded.

"I don't know Miss," said Hannah, "I put them in my bag this morning, honestly Miss, I did."

"Then where are they now you silly little girl?" A few giggles broke out when Miss Mason said this but they were instantly quelled when the angry teacher fired a stony glance that took in the whole class. Hannah stood at her desk her stomach a hard dry knot of misery.

Miss Mason stared icily at her. "You, can remain standing during this lesson Hannah and at break time you can go and see Mrs Reynolds." There was a collective gasp when Miss Mason said this. Hannah was being sent to the Headmistress; this was a sanction reserved for only the most serious of offences.

The form mistress then turned to the rest of the class and said irritably. "Could you all now please get on with your work."

Hannah stood at her desk looking foolish and feeling sick with fear. Her classmates stole furtive glances in her direction. She heard sly whisperings. She desperately wanted the lesson to be over but after this she would have to face the interview with Mrs Reynolds and, after that, the inevitable letter home to her father. Would it never end? Hannah knew that whatever trouble she might be in with the Headmistress it would be nothing compared to her father's anger. A tear plopped onto her desk. She looked down at Jerry lying in her bag.

He grinned broadly and winked.

Miss Mason was a very neat and methodical teacher. She never had anything on her desk she did not need and was never without anything she did need. Her preparation for every lesson was meticulous and thorough. For her work this afternoon she needed only one thing and that was the CD she had shown to the class that morning and had left on her desk before going to lunch. Now, as she sat down, she noticed that the disk was missing. Still angry after the incident with Hannah, she rapped her desk sharply. "Who has removed the CD from my desk?" She waited for a while and when nobody answered, said darkly. "I strongly suggest that whoever it was owns up now." Her eyes darted towards

Hannah, "Hannah do you know anything about this?" "No Miss," said Hannah, fearful that she would soon find herself in even more trouble. The angry teacher marched over to Hannah's desk.

. "Turn your bag out".

With trembling hands Hannah picked up her bag and started emptying the contents, including Jerry, onto her desk. Despairingly Miss Mason picked up Jerry and shaking him violently under Hannah's nose said. "Perhaps if you thought a bit more about your school work and a bit less about rubbish like this you wouldn't forget things and get into trouble."

She tossed Jerry on to Hannah's desk and, satisfied that the disk was not in Hannah's bag, turned angrily to the rest of the class and shouted, "All of you! Empty your bags now!" She paced up and down the aisles between the desks as bags were hurriedly emptied. At random she rummaged in bags and picked up books fanning them open as she looked for the missing disk.

Tara, who Miss Mason was now standing next to, felt a mild stab of panic; Hannah's books were in her bag. A look of alarm passed between her and her two accomplices. All around the room the girls desks were now laden with the contents of their bags. Tara was emptying her bag slowly, awkwardly trying to conceal Hannah's books among her own.

Miss Mason swooped. "What have you got there?"

"Just my books Miss," said Tara. She held them up, trying to keep Hannah's books hidden.

The disk dropped out from between the books in her hand. Tara watched open-mouthed as it clattered onto the desk in front of her and, dropping the books, scrambled to retrieve the CD.

Miss Mason stared in disbelief. "Tara!" Her voice was a mixture of disappointment and anger.

"It wasn't me Miss. Honestly Miss I don't know anything about it", said Tara picking up her empty bag and showing it to her teacher as if this somehow proved her innocence. "Someone must have put it there," she said helplessly. Miss Mason stared at her, stony faced.

It was then that Hannah timidly raised her hand. "Excuse me Miss."

"What is it now Hannah?" snapped Miss Mason.

Hannah pointed to the books on Tara's desk and almost apologetically said. "Please Miss, those are my history books."

Miss Mason, who was now beginning to lose track of what was going on, took a closer look at the books scattered on Tara's desk. "Why have you got Hannah's books?"

Tara took on the look of a trapped animal. She gaped at the books and then back at Miss Mason. Her mouth moved but no words came out. She looked wildly around the room. Sylvia and Laura looked away, not wishing to be noticed. Then without thinking, Tara blurted out. "It was a joke Miss, it was Sylvia's idea."

"No Miss," squealed Sylvia indignantly, "I just watched the door Miss, Tara and Laura took the books."

Miss Mason, now totally lost, turned to Laura and Sylvia and mustered the last of her patience. "Could someone please explain to me what is going on?"

Now Laura spoke. "I didn't know Tara took the disk Miss, I just helped her with Hannah's books," adding lamely, "it was only a joke Miss, we were going to give them back."

Hardly believing what she was hearing Miss Mason said. "A joke?" She looked at the three girls then walked back to her desk and sat down. She said nothing for a while, just shook her head very slowly and let her stern gaze wander between the three culprits. Turning to Hannah she said gently. "Sit down please Hannah," then reverted her attention back to Tara, Laura and Sylvia. "Stand up please you three." The girls stood. Miss Mason was quite calm now. "Let me get this right. You girls were going to allow me to punish Hannah for something she didn't do, is that correct?"

The three girls stood fidgeting nervously. None of them spoke.

"Is that correct!" said Miss Mason, raising her voice as her anger rose again.

"It was just a bit of fun Miss," simpered Sylvia. "We were going to give them back. Honestly Miss and I didn't know that Tara took the disk Miss."

"I didn't take the disk," said Tara, her face twisted with anxiety.

"Be quiet Tara," said Miss Mason. "At the moment I don't care about the disk. What I am concerned about is your 'bit of fun' with Hannah's books." She thought for a while and then said. "Well I'm afraid I don't find it very funny but maybe that's just because I don't have a sense of humour. So what I suggest is that the three of you pop down to Mrs Reynolds's office and see if she finds it funny."

The three girls shuffled uneasily behind their desks, none of them wanting to be the first one to move.

"Off you go," said Miss Mason. And in thrilled silence the whole class watched as the three shamed girls slunk out of the classroom.

As Hannah left school to go home that evening quite a few of the girls called out cheery goodbyes to her and two of them, girls Hannah quite liked, walked some of the way home with her and chatted happily. "See you tomorrow Hannah," they called as they parted company and a grin of pure pleasure stayed on Hannah face all the way home.

CHAPTER 17

Hannah couldn't remember ever being as happy as she was right now. She had had a lovely evening Christmas shopping with her mother and was now sitting on her bed sharing tea and chocolate biscuits with Jerry. It hardly seemed possible that only a few hours ago, miserable and in trouble at school, her whole world seemed to be coming to an end.

She listened eagerly as Jerry told her exactly what had happened that afternoon. "Well I was havin' a kip, when all of a sudden I'm wide awake and being dragged out of your bag by that one who sits in front of you. You know, the one with the face like a horse."

"Tara," said Hannah.

Jerry crammed a whole chocolate biscuit in his mouth and continued speaking showering Hannah with crumbs as he did so. "So, I've watched her and her mates as they've done a bit of jiggery-pokery with your books and then, quick as flash, I'm being shoved back in the bag again. Face down too so I can't see a bleedin' thing. Well that's given me the right hump I can tell you and I thought, right you lot, you ain't getting away with that. So when they've gone and the coast is clear I got that computer thing that was on that teacher bird's desk and stuck it in old horse face's bag and that was that."

"But why didn't you just get my books back?" said Hannah, "Then I wouldn't have got into trouble." "Yeah, but I wanted your miss whiplash to know that those nasty little mares had nicked your books, so I just left them in horse face's bag, so that when old iron-knickers Mason searches all the bags looking for the computer thing, she finds your books too."

"Oh Jerry!" said Hannah, "that's so sweet of you." Then after a moment's thought added, "but how did you know Miss Mason would go through our bags?"

"I didn't," Jerry shrugged, "I just hoped she would."

"But if she hadn't..."

"If she hadn't you'd have been bang in trouble, but she did, so it all turned out alright didn't it?"

"Well, yes I suppose so," said Hannah uneasily.

"Well that's all that matters," said Jerry. "Those three girls get a good kicking and you get to be the most popular girl in the school."

"But that was an awful risk to take."

"Yeah, but that's life ain't it," said Jerry. "The longer the odds the bigger the win."

Hannah thought for a while and then said. "Tara might even get expelled."

"Yeah and serve her right too".

Hannah considered this. "Well it certainly was a terrible spiteful thing that Tara and her friends did to me and they do deserve to be punished for that, but they are also being punished for something they didn't do."

Jerry rolled his eyes. "And you care about that?" he asked incredulously.

Hannah said nothing for a while and then, having weighed up the situation carefully, took a deep breath and said in a fairly good impersonation of Jerry's cockney twang . "Nah, serves 'em right."

Jerry threw back his head and roared with laughter. "That's my girl," he said, stuffing a celebratory biscuit in his mouth and through a hailstorm of crumbs continued. "In the Jerry Bear School of Fighting there is only one rule."

"And what's that," said Hannah giggling.

"There ain't no bleedin' rules."

Jerry and Hannah flopped back on the bed and laughed until it hurt then they laughed until they cried and then they laughed until they could laugh no more.

Hannah went to bed that night feeling that she was probably the happiest little girl in the world. And it was with thoughts of the day tumbling around her head that she drifted off into a deep, contented sleep.

CHAPTER 18

It was the dream that woke Jerry. The same one he always had, the one about the bin men. But this time it had been more disturbing, much clearer and immediate. His heart was racing and he was bathed in a sweat that chilled him through his sparse fur. He sat up and looked wildly around the dark bedroom. Hannah was asleep, her small form dimly illuminated by faint flickering moonlight.

Outside it was windy, trees creaked, doors shuddered and rain crackled against the window. The dream stayed with Jerry leaving the fear clinging to him like mud. He needed a drink.

Hannah awoke some time later. She saw Jerry's bed was empty and guessed he would be downstairs.

He was in the drawing room sitting on the big settee, holding a glass and staring into the darkness. "Are you alright?" Hannah asked settling down beside him.

"Couldn't sleep," he said flatly.

"The rain woke me up," said Hannah. "Then I saw you were gone."

"I want you to take me back to the old shop".

Hannah was stunned. "But why?"

"Because that's where I live," said Jerry. "It's my home and I'm happy there."

"But you're happy here, aren't you? We have fun. We're friends now. There's nothing back there for you. It's a horrible place."

"I belong in The Toy Shop".

Hannah studied Jerry's ugly face as he stared into his drink. He looked so troubled and sad. "It's not a toy shop Jerry," she said, "It's just a sad old place where you'll be lonely. How can you want to go back to a place where you have no friends and you have to spend your life hiding?"

"I had friends once," said Jerry, "There were toys there once."

"Yes but they're gone. They all got bought and the children gave them a life like you told me."

"But they didn't. They didn't get bought. The old man got rid of them." Jerry's eyes flashed wildly as he spoke. "I saw it all, everything."

"What?" said Hannah, shocked. "But why, why would he do such a thing?"

Jerry took a long hard drink and sat in silence.

"Please tell me Jerry, why would old Mr Jones get rid of all the toys?"

"Because he was drunk, mad drunk . . . . mad drunk after losing everything."

"Oh poor Mr Jones," whispered Hannah. "But what happened, tell me what happened."

Jerry took another drink then put the glass down. He pressed his knuckles into his eyes as if to clear his head.

"It was just before Christmas, Jones wasn't on his own in those days, he had a wife and a little girl, little Connie, she used to help her mum and dad in the shop." Jerry turned to Hannah, "how old are you?" he asked again gruffly.

"Nine".

Jerry studied Hannah for a moment and then said. "Yeah, well she was about your age. She liked to unpack the boxes when new stock came in. She'd find homes for everything and make sure all the toys were comfortable. She was a kid so she understood that us toys had feelings. Kids know that." He smiled faintly at the memory. "Well, the shop was so busy, crammed full of toys for Christmas and Old Jones was out every day getting new stock. He'd go out and his missus would stay and look after the shop. But then one morning the old boy twists his ankle and can't drive the van and the missus says she'll go to the warehouse."

Jerry's voice dropped to a whisper. "It was a horrible day, freezing and foggy. The roads were so bad." The bear shook his head. Hannah, guessing what Jerry was about to say, slipped her arm around him. "She never came back. The shop was closed over Christmas and then Old Jones opened up and ran it on his own for a while, but he'd started drinking and little Connie wasn't getting looked after properly. Then some people came to the shop, important looking people, and a lady who said she was little Connie's aunt, she came too." Jerry's voice had grown husky and thick with sadness. "It wasn't right them taking little Connie."

"Oh poor Mr Jones, poor Jerry," said Hannah. "But what happened to the toys?"

"Old Jones went mad. He tore the shop apart. Cleared the shelves and counters and chucked everything into the backyard. The toys were all out there for a couple of weeks getting rained and snowed on until everything was ruined and useless. Then the old boy shoved everything in rubbish bags and put them out for the bin men."

"Oh no!" gasped Hannah. She turned to Jerry. He was staring straight ahead his eyes now dead and hollow.

"I'll never forget the day the bin men came. I watched from the window as the crushing machine pulled up outside. It was pouring with rain and the bin men were all dressed in capes and throwing the bags from one to another and the man at the back was shouting. 'Keep 'em coming boys and the machine was making a roaring noise that sounded like the end of the world." Hannah could hardly bear to listen anymore.

"Were the other bears thrown out?"

"What other bears?"

"The ones on the box lid, your friends, the Jericho Boys."

Jerry made a small throaty grunt, as if just remembering something. "No they were all bought. I was the last one left."

Hannah thought she had never heard anything so sad. "How did you escape Jerry?" she asked choking back her tears.

"I was just lucky. When the old man was reaching in the window and grabbing everything, I got knocked down behind the shelves and that's where I stayed."

"For how long?"

Jerry shrugged. "I don't know after the bin men went the next thing I remember is the old man working in the shop selling newspapers and stuff, like he does now."

"Oh Jerry," said Hannah pulling him close to her, "no wonder you are so scared of the bin men, but that will never happen to you I would never throw you away. Please don't go back to the shop Jerry," Hannah pleaded, "stay here, you're safe here."

Jerry's voice took on a sudden harshness. "Yeah, but I don't want to be here. My life is back at the old shop, that's where I belong."

"But I've been happy since you've been here."

Jerry pulled away from Hannah and turned his back on her. "Yeah well that's tough I never asked you to buy me. I was happy with my old life and now I want it back."

Hannah didn't know what to say, and for a long time said nothing. When eventually she did speak it was simply to mumble. "I'll take you back to the old shop Jerry." Then she turned off the lamp at the end of the big settee and stared into the black nothingness of her unhappiness.

Hannah woke up cold and with that feeling of disorientation that comes with emerging from a deep sleep and finding yourself in a strange place. She couldn't understand why she wasn't in her bed and it was a few seconds before she managed to work out that she was on the settee in the sitting room and that Jerry was asleep beside her. Then she remembered why she was where she was. The conversation with Jerry came flooding back and with it an awful miserable feeling hard in the pit of her stomach. But something else was wrong too; something that had nothing to do with last night, it was something to do with now. The room was so cold. The curtains at the French windows were flapping and swirling, a pair of pale ghosts in the flickering moonlight, and there were noises. Hannah, still half asleep, felt frightened. Without thinking she turned on the table lamp and blinking in the sudden light was surprised to see the two men from the old shop, Sid and Kevin, rummaging through her father's bureau. Caught in the sudden light they froze.

"Christ! It's the bloody kid," hissed Kevin.

Hannah, too surprised to scream, simply stared at them. Sid sprang across the room and in an instant had his large hand clamped across her mouth and his face very close to hers. He whispered, "Now this, is very unfortunate, very unfortunate indeed. You've gone and put me and my mate here in a bit of a tricky situation."

"What are we going to do?" said Kevin who was now hovering nervously beside Sid.

"We're going to get out of here," said Sid.

"What about the jewellery and stuff?

"What about it?" Sid said angrily. "Are you going to hang around and look for it? Get out and get the car started. And don't make any noise. We're going to drive away from here nice and easy."

Kevin did as he was told disappearing quickly through

the French windows. Speaking very calmly, Sid said: "Now you be a good little girl, and nothing will happen to you. Okay?"

Hannah, her eyes wide with fear, did her best to nod.

"Good girl," said Sid, "now you're just coming with me for a little ride."

Hannah felt Jerry next to her and pulled him close. Sid smiled his humourless smile. "Still got your little friend I see." He nodded at Jerry. "Well, you behave and you can keep him with you." Awkwardly he gathered Hannah up in his arms keeping his hand firmly over her mouth and within seconds she was whisked out of the house and into the rainy night. Clutching Jerry she was bundled into the waiting car, which immediately sped off into the darkness. Twenty minutes later the car pulled up outside the old shop.

"Remember what I told you," Sid whispered in Hannah's ear as Kevin unlocked the shop door. "No noise." Hannah was shoved forward into the darkness. She heard the door close behind them as they followed her into the shop. Fear overwhelmed her and drained every ounce of strength from her body. It was then that Hannah's grasp on Jerry loosened. He fell to the floor and Hannah stumbled forward as she tried to retrieve him. Sid's grip tightened on her and he shook her roughly. "I'm warning you little girl," he breathed menacingly, "any trouble and it will be the worse for you." He tightened his hand over her mouth. "Open up that broom cupboard Kev. We can stick her in there."

Hannah was pushed into the inky black confines of the cupboard. "Now listen to me," said Sid, "I'm going to leave you here for a while. I'm going to lock the door so there's no point trying to get out. Understand?" Hannah nodded. "Now, I'm going to take my hand off your mouth but I warn you if you make any noise at all you'll regret it. Have you got that?" She nodded again and very slowly Sid released his grip. "Now stay here nice and quiet and you'll be okay, mess me about and you won't." Sid, turning to Kevin, said. "Start loading the car, small pricey stuff only, I want to be away from here a bit sharpish."

Then the cupboard door was shut and Hannah's darkness became total.

After Hannah had dropped him, Jerry wasted no time in scuttling behind the counter and scrambling smartly into the shop window and the safety of his hideaway. He tucked himself into his hidden corner and once he had got his breath back, heaved a deep sigh of relief. He could hardly believe his luck. He was back at home. All Jerry wanted now was for Sid and Kevin to be out of the way and then his life could get back to normal. He listened carefully; there seemed to be an awful lot of urgent activity going on out in the shop. He peeped out of the window at where Sid and Kevin's car was parked and was overjoyed to see the two men loading various goods into the boot, preparing for what looked like an imminent departure.

Once the car was loaded the two men came back into the shop closing the door behind them. Kevin spoke, his trembling voice breathless and panicky. "Is that the lot?"

"Yeah, all except the kid," replied Sid.

"Why the kid?"

"Because she's coming with us."

"Why do we have to take her, we're getting away from here aren't we?" said Kevin nervously.

"Yes but that won't make her forget us. She knows who we are and soon as we're gone she'll tell everyone who we are. We're taking her with us."

"But that's kidnapping Sid. That's heavy stuff."

Sid's anger flared. "It's kidnapping already, we've just

abducted her from her home. It's heavy stuff now and we're both in this together."

There was a silence and then Kevin said uncertainly. "So what happens now?"

"You get out there, start the car and keep the engine running. Leave the back door of the car open. When I come out I'll have the kid with me and I don't want any hold ups. Okay?"

"Okay Sid."

"Right, I'll be about five minutes. I'm going upstairs to sort out some cash with the old man first."

"You're not going to hurt him or anything are you?"

"No need," said Sid, "the old fool doesn't know anything. It's the kid who's the problem."

Safe in his hideaway in the back of the window Jerry listened to Sid and Kevin's conversation. Obviously Hannah was in serious trouble. But that, as far as Jerry was concerned, was Hannah's problem. Jerry was back at the old shop and that was exactly where he wanted to be. Sid and Kevin were clearing out which suited Jerry fine and tomorrow it would be just Jerry and the old man, just like the old days. Jerry savoured the thought of tomorrow evening. After the old man had shut the shop it would be cigarettes, beer and with any luck a curry. Jerry could hardly wait. He felt slightly bad that things weren't so good for Hannah but it was, after all, Hannah who had caused her own problems. If she hadn't come to the old shop in the first place and bought him – entirely against his will it should be remembered – then none of this would have happened. Satisfied in his own mind that he was under no obligation to help Hannah Jerry snuggled down in the rags that made up his bed.

Locked in the darkness of the small broom cupboard

Hannah could only wait. She strained her ears, desperate for any clue as to what was going on. But all she heard were odd disjointed sounds. Footsteps, at first fast then slower, a muffled voice, a word, a door closing, but mostly heavy and stifling silence. Hannah began to hope that the two men had gone, but then suddenly there were footsteps and the cupboard door was opened. The dark outline of Sid filled the doorway.

CHAPTER 19

Just as Sid had instructed him, Kevin was sitting at the wheel of the car with the engine running and the rear door open. He was nervous. The waiting was going on too long. He drummed the steering wheel with his fingers agitatedly. He had angled the rear view mirror towards the old shop door and his eyes kept flicking up hoping to see Sid. It was a wild night and when the wind gusted it blew rain through the open car door spattering the back of his neck, shredding his already strained nerves. But worst of all Kevin had the eerie sensation that someone was in the car with him. He kept turning nervously to check the back seat was empty. Kevin was seriously spooked. He looked up at the rear view mirror yet again and was relieved to see Sid and the girl coming towards the car.

Fear seemed to be all that Hannah was made of now. Sid had her arms gripped hard behind her as they walked towards the car. The tail lights glowed and the exhaust pipe fluttered white vapour into the rainy night. Hannah tried to slither from Sid's grasp. "Stupid kid," he snarled clutching her even more tightly. "Any more nonsense and I'll waste you right here and now." He shoved her roughly forward pushing her head down towards the open car door. And it was then Jerry sprang out of the car. He launched himself from where he was crouching behind the driver's seat leaping past Hannah and head butting Sid hard in the stomach, knocking the wind out of him. Sid staggered backwards and fell onto the wet pavement.

"Run for it Hannah," yelled Jerry. Following up his advantage, he jumped on Sid's face and launched a ferocious assault. He kicked, punched and gouged at Sid's eyes. "Get the old man," he shouted to Hannah as he rained blows on

Sid's head.

Hannah dodged out of the way of Sid's flailing limbs and ran blindly back to the old shop. She hammered at the door.

Jerry fought like a lion but he was too small to keep Sid down. Prising the little bear from his bleeding face Sid climbed to his feet. Still banging at the shop door Hannah turned just in time to see Sid brutally hurl Jerry into the back of the car.

"Jerry!" screamed Hannah. She was about to run back to help him but the shop door flew open and Old Jones grabbed her. "They've got Jerry," she cried trying to break free from him, but he held on to her. "It's alright, it's alright," he said, "I won't let them hurt you. You're safe now little girl." As Old Jones spoke, Hannah watched helplessly as Sid got into the car. The door slammed shut and with a squeal of tyres it drove away.

"But they've got Jerry," sobbed Hannah.

In the car Jerry and Sid continued their battle.

"What the hell is it!" screamed Kevin.

"It's that bleedin' kid's teddy bear," spluttered Sid as he fought to keep the bear at bay.

"What! Teddy bear! You're fighting a teddy bear?" Kevin looked over his shoulder and saw Jerry throw a flurry of punches at Sid.

"Get that thing outta here man," screamed Kevin. "This is freakin' me out man. This is seriously weird." The speeding car lurched dangerously across the road narrowly avoiding a lumbering rubbish truck and a gang of bin men.

"Just drive, I'm dealing with it," Sid shouted. He then hit Jerry with a mighty punch that caught the little bear just above the left eye and sent him reeling across the back seat. Sid grabbed the stunned bear by the neck and shaking him violently said. "Right, you little piece of crap, you're dead."

He wound the window down and threw Jerry out of the speeding car watching impassively as Jerry hit the hard road and rolled like a bundle of rags into a pile of rubbish bags stacked by the pavement.

Damaged and hurt Jerry lay sprawled among the black plastic bags. A cold steady rain made the tarmac gleam. Jerry felt bad. He lay still, not daring to move his broken body. There was no pain though, simply an incredible tiredness and the sensation that something was drifting away from him. He listened to the silence that surrounded him. Then, somewhere distant, he heard a deep mechanical throbbing and shortly after that, a shrill scraping and a rhythmic swish; then the voices of men. He knew what it was – the shovels and brooms of the bin men and the rumble of the rubbish truck. It was coming to get him. He wasn't dreaming. This time it was real, but Jerry felt no fear. None of this mattered. Hannah was safe, that's what mattered. Everything else was just the same old nonsense. He knew he would never have been happy at the old shop again so he might just as well be where he was now, lying in the rubbish waiting for the bin men. Gradually the distant rumble of the truck became a roar and then the huge machine was alongside him flickering the scene with amber light. "Goodbye Hannah," was the last thing Jerry said as the faceless, hooded binman scooped him up.

CHAPTER 20

Inspector Butterfield was standing with Mr and Mrs Watson on the landing outside Hannah's bedroom. He had been talking to Hannah. A big man, even in plain clothes he looked like a policeman.

"We may have to ask Hannah a few more questions," he said, "but I wouldn't worry too much if I were you. Both men have made statements and they will almost certainly be pleading guilty."

"What about the old man?" asked MrsWatson.

"Another victim madam," said the Inspector. "It seems that our two friends had been threatening him and using the shop to store their loot. They were very intimidating and the old boy was scared stiff of them. Mind you, he was pretty quick to phone us when he saw those two with Hannah."

"What will happen to him?" she asked.

The Inspector shrugged. "Well he won't be going back to the shop. We managed to contact his daughter, a Mrs Connie Freeman. She lives on the south coast and for the time being he'll be staying with her."

As the three of them spoke, they made their way downstairs.

"She's pretty tough that little girl of yours," said Inspector Butterfield as they reached the front door. Then, pausing in the doorway, he cleared his throat as if he was about to say something that required an element of tact. "When she was first interviewed by the police, Hannah made a rather unusual claim."

Mr Watson became uneasy.

"She claimed that her teddy bear had saved her."

"I think you have to remember Inspector that Hannah

117

has had quite a shock," said Mr Watson hurriedly.

The Inspector chuckled softly. "Oh please don't get me wrong sir, I'm in no way suggesting there is anything wrong with young Hannah. Far from it, one only has to talk to her to realise what a bright kiddie she is." He paused for a while and then said. "The only reason I bothered to mention the matter at all sir, is that Messer's Kevin and Sid appear to confirm her story."

"What!" said Mr Watson.

"As you can imagine," the Inspector went on, "the pair of them were both pretty shaken when we picked them up, what with having crashed the car and all, but they both said the same thing."

At this point, the Inspector produced a notebook from his top pocket and reading from it said: "It was that bloody bear. It attacked me," Inspector Butterfield looked up from his book and then said in his best comic policeman's voice. "The defendant then showed me various facial cuts and abrasions that pointed to him having suffered a particularly violent assault."

Mr Watson gaped at the police officer and then laughed nervously. When he eventually did manage to speak he simply said rather desperately. "You don't believe them do you?"

The Inspector laughed out loud. "What those two villains? I wouldn't believe them if they told me the right time." He then looked Mr Watson squarely in the eye and gripping his arm said in a deadly serious voice, "but I do believe your daughter sir."

The Inspector opened the front door and after the traditional "goodnight sir, goodnight madam," made his way to the waiting squad car. He was about to get into the car when Mrs Watson called after him, "Inspector

Butterfield, please wait. Tell me why you believe Hannah?"

"Your daughter isn't a liar. Simple as that." His eyes twinkled kindly.

"What about the bear. Was he found?"

Butterfield's face darkened. He shook his head, "I'm sorry, it seems the street cleaners got there before us." The Inspector got into the car. "Goodnight madam," he said again, and the car pulled away.

Mrs Watson wandered back into the house pondering what the policeman had just said.

"What a strange thing to say," she said turning to her husband. "What do you think he meant?"

"I haven't the foggiest idea," he replied, "but it's small wonder that the criminals seem to be taking over with officers like him around" and giving one of his more dismissive tuts shook his head.

"But don't you think it's a coincidence George, those two men saying that about the bear? You know, confirming what Hannah has been saying."

Mr Watson stared open mouthed at his wife. "What! I honestly can't believe what I'm hearing. But if you must know, what I think is this. I think that PC plod out there has lost the plot completely. I think Hannah needs to see more of Dr Kingston. And I think you are suffering from shock. Or at least I hope you are."

Hannah listened to all this from the landing. Once she would have been crushed by what her father had said but Jerry had changed all that. If no one gives you a life then you have to make one for yourself. That was the simple truth Jerry had taught her. He had made his own life and lived it on his own terms and now Hannah would do the same. Today she would cry for Jerry but tomorrow she would just get on with things.

CHAPTER 21

It was Christmas Eve and Mr Watson was in a more than usually bad mood. He had just got home from the office. "Every bloody year it's the same, everything stops for Christmas. They ought to ban it or at least cut it down to once every four years like the World Cup. It's a complete waste of time at work. No one's got their mind on the job. They only come in to go to the pub." He shook his head uncomprehendingly. Looking at his watch he said. "God, is that the time, one-o-clock? I've got so much to do."

Mrs Watson eyed her husband suspiciously. "You are going to help me with the last of the shopping aren't you George? Thomas is staying here with Hannah and I really can't manage it all on my own."

"Yes, yes," he said irritably, "I've got a meeting this afternoon but that won't take long and after that I'm free to give a hand."

"A meeting! But it's Christmas Eve George. I thought you were taking the rest of the day off."

"What have I just been saying? Christmas, Christmas, damn Christmas, the whole world goes mad over a couple of days holiday."

"It's not just a couple of days holiday," his wife said patiently, "it's a chance for us to be together. And this year, especially after what has happened to Hannah, I thought you would realise that."

"Yes, well I'm afraid something important has come up which I have to attend to. For God's sake it's not the end of the world. You make a start on the shopping and I'll meet you later. You don't need me there all the time surely."

Mrs Watson considered protesting but knew it would be a waste of time. Instead she said quietly. "No George, but it would have been nice to do something together."

George Watson either didn't hear this last remark or chose to ignore it. Looking at his watch again he said. "We'd better hurry my meeting's in half an hour."

Twenty-five minutes later, much to Mrs Watson's surprise, she and her husband were pulling up outside the old shop. It was closed and looked even shabbier and more run-down than the last time she had seen it. There was a big sign nailed to the wall by an upstairs window. It read, Watson and Co and slashed across it was a banner saying, "Sold."

George looked up at the sign grinning, what his wife called his fat cat grin, and handed her the car keys. "If you pop down to the High Street, I'll meet you there in about an hour."

Mrs Watson tilted her head towards the old shop and asked. "What's going on George?"

Mr Watson's grin became a self-satisfied smirk. "I'm buying this place, I had a feeling about it the first time I saw it, you know the day we went to the Antiques Fair."

Mrs Watson suddenly felt very tired. She gazed out of the car window at the deserted street. It had started to snow, small mean flakes that gave the whole scene a feeling of intense loneliness. "Is that why we've hardly seen you at home recently?"

"I do have a business to run Angela and deals like this require a little delicate negotiation and a lot of personal attention"

His wife felt anger and disgust well up inside her. "When you say 'deals like this', I assume you mean you got it cheap?"

"Of course, that's business. Buy cheap and sell dear. I can get two flats out of this place. And a wine bar or restaurant on the ground floor."

Mrs Watson was finding it difficult to control her voice but managed to say. "You have children George and one, I might remind you, has just been through a very traumatic experience and who would have liked to have seen a bit more of you."

"Good God Angela, what do you want me to do? Neglect my business?"

"No George, I would never expect you to do that. Neglect your daughter, that's much easier isn't it?"

"I can't let deals like this pass me by, the old fool didn't have a clue what the place was worth and couldn't wait to get rid of it. Do you realise how much money we'll make out of this?"

Mrs Watson put her hands to her ears and shook her head furiously. "We won't make any money George. You can make as much as you like. I don't want any of it. Not if you're telling me that you couldn't be bothered to spend some time with Hannah because you were too busy cheating some poor old man. An old man who, I might remind you again, helped Hannah when she was in trouble. You can keep your grubby money."

He was taken aback by this attack. "Steady on Angela. You're making me sound like a monster. I've done the best I can for Hannah. I'm going to pay for her to see Dr Kingston twice a week aren't I?"

His wife's patience snapped. "Shut up George!" Furious, she lunged across the car and pushing open the driver's door, gave her husband a violent shove.

"Have you gone mad woman?" said George, trying not to fall out of the car.

"Get out! Get out. Get out and do your rotten deal." She gave another mighty push and he fell clumsily into the road.

She quickly slammed the car door shut and pushed down the lock.

Jumping to his feet George banged angrily on the car window. "Are you out of your mind? Let me in."

Angela clambered awkwardly into the driver's seat and lowered the window a couple of inches. "Hannah needed you. She loved that stupid bear and now it's gone and I know you can't bring it back, but you could have at least given her some support."

"Oh no," he groaned. "Not all that bloody teddy bear nonsense again. Can't you see you're only going to make her worse? Just ignore her, let Dr Kingston sort her out."

"Sort what out? What exactly is wrong with her loving her teddy bear George? What is so dreadful about it that she needs to see a psychiatrist."

"She thought it was alive Angela," he said desperately. "No, no, it was worse than that, she actually believed it was alive. And it was because of all that teddy bear nonsense she ended up getting in trouble. She needs professional help and that's what Dr Kingston will give her."

"What Hannah needs," his wife said coldly, "is a father. But maybe a stuffed toy was the best she could hope for."

Realising that, locked out of the car as he was, his bargaining position was somewhat weak, Mr Watson became more conciliatory. "Okay, okay," he held up his hands. "Let me just get this meeting out of the way, then what we'll do is go and buy her a new bear. Okay? Now open the door please, it's freezing out here and I need my briefcase."

"A new bear won't help George. Hannah is grieving for Jerry"

Mr Watson gave a sudden snort of laughter.

"You think it's funny George?"

"I'm sorry," he said, "It just sounded funny, you calling it Jerry like that. Anyone would think you thought the bear was alive too."

"I wish I did," said Mrs Watson bitterly. "I wish I believed like Hannah, but I can't. But what I can do is to believe in Hannah."

"Oh come on now, surely you can't mean that, it's insane."

Mrs Watson said nothing for a while. She pressed her hands hard into her eyes then, without emotion, said, "I've had enough George. I think the best thing is that I do the shopping and then go straight home. You do what you like." She put the car in gear.

"But how am I going to get home?"

"Don't bother coming home George, I don't want you at home." She shook her head furiously trying to smother the rage she was feeling. And then, letting go of some of it she turned and said, "I mean it George, don't you dare come home."

CHAPTER 22

Moses had spent Christmas Eve helping Linda in the flower shop. They had opened early that morning and had been very busy all day long. And now they were both pleasantly exhausted and looking forward to spending the Christmas holiday together. A biting wind drove swirling snow along the broad pavement and they huddled together in the shop doorway as Moses locked the door.

It was Moses that noticed the man leaning unsteadily on the railings. He thought at first he must be a drunk, a refugee from one of the many pubs and wine bars that littered the High Street. It was a common enough sight on Christmas Eve. Nonetheless Moses was concerned and went over to him. Resting his hand gently on the man's shoulder, he asked. "Are you okay mister?"

The man straightened himself and turning towards Moses said. "Fine thank you." He smiled gratefully. "Just a bit chilly that's all. I'm on my way home now." The man went to walk away but without the support of the railings, became unsteady and swayed dangerously. Moses held his arm. "Hey mister, are you sure you're okay?" Steadying himself the man said. "I'm fine, really I'm fine. I just need to get home." He smiled at Moses again. "You're very kind have a Merry Christmas."

Moses smiled back. "Yeah, you too, Merry Christmas."

The man studied Moses's face. His broad friendly smile had stirred a memory. "You're the Big Issue seller," he said.

Moses nodded, "I used to be. Do I know you?"

The man shook his head. "You helped my daughter a little while ago and I never thanked you."

Moses studied him, "I do know you," he said, "You're Hannah's dad."

At that moment the wind gusted an arctic blast. This chilled Mr Watson through to the bone making him feel colder than he could ever remember being before. He suddenly felt his body had no substance and his legs buckled under him. As he fell forward Moses grabbed him. Turning to Linda in the shop doorway he shouted urgently. "Linda, its Hannah's dad. Open up the shop. Quickly, he's in trouble."

It was seven thirty when the phone rang. Hannah answered it hoping it would be her father. It wasn't. When a voice, that she didn't immediately recognise, said "Hannah?" she answered hesitantly.

"Yes."

"Hannah, It's Moses."

"Moses!" exclaimed Hannah, pleased that it was him, but at the same time disappointed that it wasn't her father.

"Hannah sweetheart," said Moses urgently, "I need to talk to your mummy and it's very important."

Her mother was already at Hannah's side. Puzzled, Hannah said. "It's my friend Moses, the man that looked after me when I bought Jerry. He wants to speak to you."

Mrs Watson couldn't imagine what Moses, a man she had never met, would want to speak to her about, so when she answered there was a certain caution in her voice. "Hello."

"Mrs Watson," said Moses, "look I'm sorry to bother you like this on Christmas Eve, but I've got your husband with me and....."

She cut him short. "What's wrong?"

"Nothing, nothing at all," said Moses reassuringly, "but he does need to see you."

Mrs Watson paused for a long time before she spoke and then said. "I appreciate you calling Mr Moses but I don't think I have much to say to my husband at the moment.

Though I would like to thank you for what you did for Hannah the other week, I should have thanked you before but we've had a bit of trouble and...."

"I know all about that," said Moses, "and it doesn't matter. But if you really want to thank me for helping Hannah, then please do as I ask. Go to the old shop and be sure to take Hannah and Thomas with you."

"What, now?"

"Right away," said Moses, "please. It's really important." Then he hung up.

Mrs Watson had meant what she had said when she had told her husband not to come home, but that had been over five hours ago. Now though she was missing him, and the children were missing him, and it was, after all, Christmas Eve. But what was going on? Why was Moses phoning and not George? Probably because he knew she wouldn't speak to him. Thomas and Hannah waited expectantly for their mother to say something. She looked into both their faces, Hannah with all her troubles but still getting on with things, Thomas, sullen and uncaring on the surface but underneath desperate to see his sister happy. Mrs Watson took her coat from the hallstand. "We've got to go out."

"Where to?" said Thomas.

"To the old shop. Daddy's there."

Hannah sat next to Thomas in the cosy darkness of the car staring out of the window at the snowy night. What, she wondered, could be the connection between her father and Moses and why were they going to the old shop? She began to feel excited. Something, she was sure, was about to happen. Issues were about to be resolved, maybe for good, maybe for bad. Fearing disappointment she concentrated on the thing that she wanted most - for her father to come home and for the family to spend Christmas together. She dare not wish for any more so she held onto this one thought while the car passed through the wintry streets.

When they pulled up outside the old shop everyone was surprised to see it lit up. The softly glowing windows cast a warm glow on the snowy pavement making the whole scene look story-book Christmassy. The shop door opened almost immediately and Mr Watson came out and got into the car.

"What on earth are you wearing?" said Mrs Watson.

"My clothes got wet," said Mr Watson looking down at the outrageously baggy track-suit.

Suddenly anxious, Mrs Watson asked. "Are you alright? You're not ill are you?"

"I'm fine. I promise you I'm fine," said Mr Watson. "And right now, how I am is not the issue. I have a few things I need to say to all of you, important things." He turned and smiled at Thomas and Hannah. "You okay kids?"

"Are you coming home dad?" said Thomas.

"Why are you here daddy?" said Hannah, "why did Moses phone?"

Their father held his hands up. "If you'll just hear me out I'll tell you everything and then you'll all know what happened today. Then you guys and mum can decide what's going to happen. Is that okay?" Hannah and Thomas nodded.

George turned to his wife. "When you and I parted company this afternoon you drove off with my briefcase and my overcoat." Mrs Watson went to speak but her husband stopped her. "You don't need to say anything. It served me right. In fact it was the best thing that could have happened to me. My cheque book, credit cards, cash cards and cash were all in the case and my phone was in my overcoat pocket."

"Oh no," gasped Mrs Watson.

"I had about five quid in change on me so I went and bought a newspaper and had a couple of cups of coffee and then I tried to call you from a call box and couldn't get through and then I had another cup of coffee and suddenly my money was all gone. So I got angry and stomped around the shops for a while. Then I tried to get a taxi but that was impossible and then the weather was getting worse and pretty soon it was dark and a blizzard was blowing and my feet were wet."

"Oh how awful for you," said his wife.

George continued. "Then I thought I'd see if I could get on a tube-train, but I was at the other end of the High Street and it was such a long walk to the station I got really cold and began to feel a bit weird."

"Poor daddy," said Hannah.

"Lucky daddy," said Mr Watson. "By pure chance I stopped outside your friend Linda's shop just as she and Moses were locking up. They saw I was in trouble and they took me into the shop to thaw me out. Then they took me to their home and Moses lent me these huge clothes."

"Oh George how kind of them to help you," said Mrs Watson.

"That's exactly what I thought. How kind of these people to help a man they hardly knew. I feel like I've had a wake up call. I felt ashamed because I knew that I wouldn't have helped me. I'd have just walked by."

Mrs Watson put her hand on her husband's. "I don't think so George. I married a nice man and I know he's never been far away."

Mr Watson turned to Hannah and said brightly. "Would you like to see Linda and Moses, Hannah?"

"When?" said Hannah excitedly.

"Right now," he said getting out of the car.

"What, they're here?"

"Right here and waiting to see you." He held open the car door. "Why don't we all go in and say hello."

CHAPTER 23

Hannah peered round the door of the old shop. It looked so different. Lit by what must have been a hundred candles it was magical, altered beyond recognition from the dark frightening place that she remembered. And there, behind the counter, were Moses and Linda beaming at her. People from another life, almost strangers but so close to Hannah's heart that she felt she had known them forever. It was wonderful to see them again but it made her want to cry. And then there were thoughts of Jerry cramming into her head and that made her want to cry too. So she cried because she knew she couldn't stop herself. For now though, she decided she was crying because she was happy. Too many good things were happening now and she wanted to savour all of them.

Earlier, the only thing that Hannah had wanted was for her family to be together for Christmas and that was happening. If she had dared to wish for anything more it would have been that her father would be nicer. Now, even that seemed possible.

When the hugs of reunion and the kisses of thanks were over, Mr Watson, looking ridiculous in Moses huge tracksuit, took centre stage in the old shop and addressing everyone said. "It's Christmas Eve and I guess we all want to get home, but I've got a few things I need to say and I know Moses has got some news for us." He turned to Moses and Linda. "Shall I go first?"

"Go ahead George," said Moses. "The floor is yours."

"First of all," said Mr Watson turning to his wife, "I think you will be pleased to know that I have spoken to Mr Jones and told him that after the holiday I will be getting an independent estate agentin to value the property and that I will be paying him whatever they deem to be a fair market price."

"I'm proud of you George," she said.

"And," he continued, "I'm not going to convert it into flats either. I've had a better idea. What this place needs to be is what it used to be, a proper toyshop selling proper toys. You know, train sets and dolls and rocking horses and dolls houses, real toys that last, that children can actually play with. And it should also be a place where children can get their toys mended."

"What! You're going to run a toyshop daddy," said Hannah, "and mend toys as well?"

"Of course not," grinned Mr Watson, "I'd be hopeless. And anyway the kids would all hate me. And before anyone thinks I'm going soft let me just say that I'm not doing this because I'm a nice bloke. I'm doing it because it makes better business sense for me to retain the shop as an asset than to sell it. But of course someone will need to run it, so I've asked Moses to become my business partner and to manage the business."

"Really!" gasped Hannah, "Moses will be working here."

Her father nodded.

"Can I have a Saturday job?" said Thomas eagerly to his father.

"You'll have to ask Moses," said Mr Watson, "as I said, he's the man in charge."

"Can I Moses?" said Thomas.

"Of course you can," said Moses, "you can be my right hand man."

"And can I come and visit?" said Hannah.

"Of course."

"But what about your magazines Moses, won't you sell them anymore?" asked Hannah.

When Hannah said this she noticed Moses and her father had exchanged a glance. She didn't know what this meant, but the tummy fluttering feeling that she had experienced earlier in the car returned, only this time more forcefully. Outside, snow had started to fall again, adding even further to the Christmas card quality of the evening and her almost unbearable feeling of excitement and anticipation.

Her father spoke. "I said earlier that Moses had some news for us all and I think now is a good time for me to hand over to him."

Moses, who was leaning on the counter, drew himself up to his full height. "Well Hannah, I stopped being a Big Issue guy pretty much after that day I met you. Thanks to you I met Linda and thanks to Linda I met her brother and thanks to him I got myself a job."

"Oh Moses," said Hannah, I'm so pleased. "Is it a nice job?"

"It's a lovely job Hannah and I work with a really good bunch of guys, but its night work and because of that I don't get to see much of Linda, so working in The Toy Shop is going to be much better for us. And anyway, the job that Linda's brother got me was only a temporary one, just for the Christmas period. But I'll tell you all about that later." Moses turned to Linda. "You'd better get our surprise guest," he said. And from behind the counter Linda produced the bear.

"Jerry!" Hannah screamed.

"My God!" cried Mrs Watson. "Is it really him?"

Hannah rushed forward and Linda handed Jerry to her. "It is him," she said holding the bear close to her and studying his ugly, mute, face. She grinned at him and felt his small furry paw give her arm a sly squeeze, "It really is Jerry.

But how? I thought he was dead. The Inspector said the bin men got him."

"They did," said Moses laughing, "but luckily the bin man was me. That was my Christmas job. Linda's brother is a big shot guy at the council and he got me a place on the gang that works the market. I found Jerry all beaten up and soaking wet in a big pile of rubbish sacks."

"You must have wondered how on earth he got there," said Mrs Watson.

"I did and when I took him home Linda and I were both worried about Hannah. We couldn't even begin to imagine what had happened. But we couldn't contact anyone. We didn't know anything about Hannah. So we just cleaned Jerry up and hoped that Hannah would come and see us one day. Of course we never imagined that Hannah had had such an adventure, not until George told us all about it this evening."

"Oh thank you so much for looking after him," said Hannah.

"That's okay sweetheart," said Linda, "it was no trouble".

"Then he's behaved himself while he's been staying with you?" asked George.

"Of course," said Linda, "why wouldn't he?"

"Because," he said, "for the short time that he lived with us we had nothing but trouble."

"Really," said Linda, not sure how serious Mr Watson was being.

"Really". He took Jerry from Hannah and stroked the few thin strands of hair on the bear's head. "He certainly stirred things up when he was with us."

Outside the snow was falling thicker than ever and from somewhere distant carol singers could be heard. Mr Watson turned and looked at the happy faces that surrounded him and could hardly believe how happy this made him feel. It was a new experience. He held Jerry up and staring into the bear's dull glazed eyes said. "Merry Christmas Jerry." And he could have sworn the bear winked at him.

Want to know what happens next?

The Big Apple and Charlie Large

Published Autumn 2009